LITTLE LEAGUE

DISTRICT

DOUBLE-

HEADER

MATT CHRISTOPHER

(L)(B)
Little, Brown and Company
New York   Boston

Copyright © 2013 by Matt Christopher Royalties, Inc.

Little, Brown and Company

Hachette Book Group
237 Park Avenue, New York, NY 10017
Visit our website at www.lb-kids.com
www.mattchristopher.com

Little, Brown and Company is a division of Hachette Book Group, Inc.
The Little, Brown name and logo are trademarks of Hachette Book Group, Inc.

The publisher is not responsible for websites (or their content)
that are not owned by the publisher.

First Edition: July 2013

Matt Christopher® is a registered trademark of Matt Christopher Royalties, Inc.

Little League Baseball, Little League, the medallion and the keystone are registered trademarks and service marks belonging exclusively to Little League Baseball, Incorporated.

© 2013 Little League Baseball, Incorporated. All Rights Reserved.

Text written by Stephanie True Peters

Library of Congress Cataloging-in-Publication Data

Peters, Stephanie True, 1965–
    District doubleheader / Matt Christopher ; [text written by Stephanie True Peters].—1st ed.
        p. cm.—(Little league ; [2])
    "A Little League Book."
    Summary: "Cousins Liam and Carter work hard to earn positions on their regional All-Star baseball teams"—Provided by publisher.
    ISBN 978-0-316-22043-9
    [1. Baseball—Fiction. 2. Cousins—Fiction.] I. Christopher, Matt. II. Title.
    PZ7.P441835Dis 2013
    [Fic]—dc23

                                                                    2012040489

10   9   8   7   6   5   4   3   2   1

RRD-C

Printed in the United States of America

The Little League® Pledge

I trust in God

I love my country

And will respect its laws

I will play fair

And strive to win

But win or lose

I will always do my best

CHAPTER

"Look who's here."

Liam McGrath, starting catcher for the Pythons in their game against the Cobras, glanced sideways at his teammate Rodney Driscoll. Rodney ran his hand over his tight black curls and then jerked his chin toward the bleachers. Liam looked over and his mouth tightened.

"Phillip DiMaggio," he muttered. "Great. What's he doing here?"

Rodney shrugged. "Taking in a game? Checking out the competition? Trying to decide who to vote for as an All-Star?"

Liam flinched at the mention of the vote. He'd been an All-Star last year and wanted to be one again this year.

But he didn't think that was likely. Last year he'd been a leader, a player teammates turned to when the pressure was on. Now he was the new kid in town, an unknown. Or worse, known for something he wished no one knew.

He twisted his Pythons baseball cap around so the brim covered his neck and pulled his catcher's helmet into place over his face and throat guard.

He knew he shouldn't be surprised to see Phillip. After all, they lived in the same town now. Played in the same local Little League, too, although for different teams, thankfully. If he had been assigned to DiMaggio's team, he didn't know what he would have done.

Yes, I do. I would have played, he thought, *because I'm not a quitter.* But it wouldn't have been easy seeing his nemesis at practices every week, and having to cheer him on during games, and maybe even—Liam gulped at the thought—catching for him.

Liam and Phillip had first met the previous August at the Little League Baseball World Series in Williamsport, Pennsylvania. At that time, Liam was still living in Pennsylvania, close to his cousin and best friend, Carter Jones. That summer, he, Carter, and their All-Star teammates had accomplished an amazing feat: They had beaten all the other teams from the Mid-Atlantic Region to earn a berth at the World Series. They had won the majority of their games in the World Series tournament, too, and advanced to the U.S. Championship.

Their opponent in that game was a Southern California team representing the West Region. The West's pitcher was Phillip DiMaggio.

Liam had no clue who DiMaggio was then, but Carter did. He'd had a run-in with the pitcher during Little League Baseball Camp the summer before. And two days before the United States Championship, Carter told Liam all about it.

"Because of his last name, I thought he was related to the great Joe DiMaggio." Carter scrubbed his hands over his face. "So I asked him to autograph my camp jersey. But of course, I had forgotten Joltin' Joe doesn't have any direct heirs. Phillip called me Number One Fan the rest of camp—he thought it was hysterical. I thought it was humiliating."

When Carter told him the story, Liam didn't get mad. In fact, he said it probably helped Carter to use his anger at Phillip as motivation to become a better pitcher. Still, he didn't like the trick Phillip had pulled. The first time Liam came face-to-face with DiMaggio, Liam played a prank of his own. He poked a spot on the pitcher's shirt and told him he had a stain. When Phillip looked down, Liam jerked his finger up, bopped Phillip in the nose, and chortled, "Made you look!"

That innocent prank came back to haunt him during the U.S. Championship Game.

Mid-Atlantic was down a run in the bottom of the sixth. Phillip was on the mound. Liam came up to bat. There was a runner on third, two outs. Liam let the first pitch go by for a called strike. He nicked the second for a foul and strike two. Determined to hit a game-winning homer off DiMaggio, he took a monstrous swing at the third pitch—and missed.

Worse than missed. He swung so hard that he corkscrewed around off-balance and fell face-first into the dirt. In front of thousands of spectators. On live television.

Game over.

Moments later, Phillip offered him a hand to help him up. To the viewers watching at home, the gesture looked like the epitome of sportsmanship. But the cameras and microphones missed something. With a flick of his outstretched finger, Phillip brushed Liam's shirt and then touched the batter's nose.

"Hey, McGrath," he whispered, pointing at Liam. "Made you whiff!"

Back home, Liam had tried to remember everything good that had happened during the World Series and to put that one bad moment behind him. But that was easier said than done. First, he discovered that a video clip of his strikeout was available for viewing by anyone who had access to the Internet. Second, he learned that his family was moving across the country to Southern California. Third, and most unbelievable, he found out that he would now be living in the same town as Phillip DiMaggio.

Liam risked another glance at the stands. He panned over the spectators—an older man with a stern expression and almond-shaped eyes, a pair of girls giggling together, a group of parents—then landed on Phillip. His brown eyes met the pitcher's jet-black ones for a brief moment. Then Phillip looked away.

Liam adjusted his leg guards and hurried out onto the field.

He'd survived moving across the country, leaving all his friends. If he'd been put on the same team as DiMaggio, he would have survived that, too. No, better than survived. He would have succeeded.

Last August, it was game over, he thought. *From here on out, it's game on.*

CHAPTER

Carter Jones bagged the pile of leaves he'd been raking and carried it to the parking lot. It was Little League Cleanup Day, and along with dozens of other players, parents, and Little League coaches, he was getting the baseball fields ready for the upcoming season.

"Hustle over, everyone. Team meeting!" Mr. Harrison, coach of the Hawks, called. A wiry man with thick black hair, he had been Carter and Liam's coach last year and throughout the All-Star team's run in the postseason. Carter counted himself very lucky to have been drafted to his team again this time around. It took some of the sting out of being separated from Liam.

Some, but not all. Until Liam moved, he and Carter

were inseparable. They were the same age, had the same friends, and went to the same school. They slept at each other's houses, shared meals, and celebrated every birthday and holiday together.

They played baseball together, too, and were teammates from Little League Tee Ball all the way up through the Major Division. When Carter began pitching regularly on their Majors team, Liam became his catcher. They proved to be a formidable duo on the field.

"It's like you can read each other's minds," a fellow player once marveled.

Carter thought that wasn't far from the truth. Maybe he and Liam didn't have an actual psychic link like in science-fiction books, but they did share a connection that was stronger than most. And now that the Little League season was about to begin, Carter missed his cousin more than ever.

In the dugout, a blond-haired boy named Ash La-Brie waved Carter over. "Got room here."

Carter hesitated before taking the seat. He liked Ash but felt disloyal to Liam whenever he hung out with him. For one thing, Ash and his mother had moved into Liam's old house. Now Ash ate in Liam's kitchen, hung out in Liam's living room, and slept in Liam's bedroom. As if that wasn't weird enough, he had also taken over Liam's position as Carter's catcher. Ash was good behind the plate, no doubt, but...well, he wasn't Liam and that was that.

Coach Harrison opened the meeting by thanking them for their hard work. "The concession stand now has a nice new coat of paint. And apparently, so do some of you!"

The players who had been painting looked at their blue flecked clothing and laughed.

"Hmm," the coach continued, noting a similar smudge of paint on his arm, "guess 1 should have said 'some of *us*.' And now some more good news. The Hawks are adding a new player to their roster."

He looked toward the parking lot. "Ah, there's your new teammate now!"

He pointed to a person jogging across the field. The kid's cap was shading his face, so it was only when he reached the dugout that everyone realized—

"It's a *girl*!" shortstop Arthur Holmes blurted out.

Carter was surprised, too. He knew Little League Baseball was open to boys and girls; still, actually having a girl on the team was unexpected.

"Everyone, please welcome Rachel Warburton," the coach said. "She just got called up from the Minors."

That's when Carter finally recognized her. They'd been in the same class in fourth grade. Back then, she had worn her long brown hair loose and had a quick, easy grin that invited everyone near her to smile back. Her hair was shorter now and tucked through her cap. But when she saw him, that same grin lit up her face.

"Hey, Carter!" she said. "Got room for me?"

Carter blushed, embarrassed at being singled out, but said, "Uh, sure." He nudged Ash. Ash gave him a look and then slid over.

Rachel sat between them and whispered, "I watched the whole World Series last year. You were awesome!"

Carter reddened even more. "Thanks."

"I was sorry to hear Liam moved away. That must be terrible for—"

"Hey, do you guys mind?" Ash interrupted tersely. "The coach is talking."

Carter immediately snapped his attention back to Mr. Harrison. The coach reminded them they were expected to attend all practices. He also assured them they would each see playing time in every game.

"Finally, remember that win or lose, you support your fellow Hawks and congratulate your opponents. Understood?"

Cheers rose from the kids on the bench.

The meeting ended then. But before Carter could return to his job, the coach called him over. "You too, Ash," he added.

Then he said something that took Carter completely by surprise. "I've been thinking about your curveball."

At Ash's urging, Carter had experimented with that pitch. He thought he was throwing it well, too, and hoped to add it to his pitching arsenal when the season began.

When Coach Harrison found out about it, however, he'd made his disapproval clear. He told Carter that the curve could damage a young pitcher's arm. While Little League didn't outright forbid the pitch, he let Carter know that he certainly didn't want any of his pitchers throwing it. Carter had dropped the curve then and there—much to Ash's displeasure.

"I still don't want you to throw the curveball," the coach said now. "However, I wonder if you'd like some help on your knuckleball instead?"

Carter's green eyes widened. He'd tried the knuckleball before without much success, but he was sure he could master it with Coach Harrison's help. "Absolutely! You tell me when and where, and I'll be there!"

"It won't be me," Mr. Harrison corrected. "A new

volunteer in the league, Mark Delaney, is running a pitching clinic Monday evening at the high school. He needs catchers, too," he added, looking at Ash. "If he likes what he sees, he'll spend time with you on the knuckleball. So, I take it you're interested?"

"Absolutely!" Carter said again.

"Me too," Ash said.

"Me three!"

Carter turned in surprise. He hadn't heard Rachel approach, but there she was, standing behind him and looking at the coach hopefully.

Ash narrowed his eyes. "*You* want to pitch?"

"Heck, I want to try playing anywhere and everywhere," she said, "except 'left out'!"

The joke was completely lame and yet Carter laughed. So did the coach.

"Then you should attend, too," Mr. Harrison said. "Never hurts to have another hurler in the bull pen. Right, boys?"

"Right!" Carter said.

Ash murmured something, too. But whether he was agreeing with the coach, Carter couldn't be sure.

CHAPTER

THREE

Ball three!" the umpire behind Liam called.

"Time!" Coach Driscoll shouted from the dugout.

The umpire stood up and waved his hands through the air.

Liam pushed his mask back and jogged to the mound to talk to Spencer Park. The pitcher was on the verge of walking another batter, his fourth in three innings. There were two outs and the Pythons had a two-run lead. But it wouldn't take much to even out that score.

"Hey, man," Liam said, keeping his voice calm. "Take a moment. Get your focus back and—yo, you with me?"

Spencer's almond-shaped eyes had shifted toward the bleachers. Now they darted back to Liam. "I just get nervous when he's here," he confessed. "I want to impress him, you know? But every game he comes to, I pitch wild."

Liam figured Spencer had been looking at Phillip DiMaggio. After all, who else in the stands could make him so jittery? Well, it was up to Liam to take those jitters away. He laid a hand on the pitcher's shoulder. Spencer was shorter than he was by at least two inches, a reminder to Liam that he was a year younger—and in his first season with the Majors.

"Listen," Liam said, locking his gaze with Spencer's, "you're not here to impress anybody. You're here to get these Cobras to swing at your pitches. So put him"—he nodded toward DiMaggio—"out of your mind. That's what—"

"Let's go, Pythons," the umpire cut in.

Liam had been about to say that he'd been trying to put DiMaggio out of his own mind. At the umpire's call, however, he immediately hustled back to the plate. He knew that some officials appreciated a quick response to their commands. Sure enough, this umpire gave him an approving nod.

The brief pep talk seemed to have helped, for Spencer's next pitch came right down the heart of the plate. Liam assumed the Cobra would let it go by—the first three pitches were balls, after all, so the odds of a fourth were in his favor—but the player swung and connected for a weak grounder toward Clint Kelley. The husky shortstop fielded the ball cleanly and threw to Reggie Zimmer at first base. The Cobra was out, and the top of the inning was over.

Reggie, first up for the Pythons, strode to the plate. An on-again, off-again hitter with a perpetual slouch to his shoulders, Reggie blasted the second pitch into right field for a double that drew whoops from his teammates. Alex Kroft and Robert Hall made outs, and then Spencer clipped four fouls down the first-base line.

But on the fifth pitch—*pow!* Spencer may have been short, but his hit went long, a sizzling line drive that found the right-center field gap. He raced down the base path, touched the bag, and kept going. Luckily, Reggie had abandoned second for third. When the dust settled, both runners were safe.

Then Rodney came up to bat. It was almost impossible to see his expression beneath the protective helmet, but Liam bet it was full of determination. The chatter from the bench rose to a fever pitch.

"Here you go, Rodney. Here you go!"

"Knock the cover off that ball!"

"Bring 'em home, man. Bring 'em home!"

There was power behind such cheers, Liam knew. He used to hear them all the time back in Pennsylvania—

especially last year. He'd been one of the most feared hitters in the league. Whenever he came up to bat, his teammates would stomp and yell, the outfield would back up, and then, when the pitch came in—

Crack!

For a brief moment, Liam's daydream had been so real, he thought *he'd* hit the ball.

"Yes, sir, that's my bro!" Sean Driscoll bellowed, leaping up and punching the air with a freckled fist.

Rodney's scorching blast scored Reggie and Spencer. Then he crossed home plate and trotted into the dugout, where the Pythons swarmed him.

As Liam slapped his friend on the back, he caught sight of the Cobras pitcher. The boy's shoulders were bowed in defeat. Liam felt a stab of sympathy for him.

Not everyone on the team felt the same way.

"Man, I can't wait to take another crack at him."

Robert's voice was low but full of glee. A big kid with a thick neck and wide mouth that turned down at the corners, he reminded Liam of a bullfrog. He was Liam's least favorite teammate, a complainer who pointed fingers at everyone but himself when something went wrong and reveled in other people's weaknesses.

Liam had a more personal reason for disliking Robert, though. Robert was friends with Phillip. At baseball tryouts, he'd recognized Liam as the player DiMaggio had struck out in the World Series—and then started calling Liam a nickname based on that moment: Major Whiff.

Coach Driscoll glanced at Robert. For a moment, Liam thought he'd heard the mean comment about the Cobras pitcher. But the coach was at the far end of the dugout. He would have needed supersonic hearing to pick up on it.

Liam considered saying something but didn't. *It would be my word against Robert's,* he thought. He knew nothing busted up a team faster than animosity in the dugout. So he kept what he'd heard under wraps.

After giving up the home run, the Cobras pitcher rallied and struck out Clint to end the inning. The Cobras failed to get on the board during their turn at bat, though, so the score remained 7–2.

Liam was the Pythons leadoff batter for the bottom of the fourth inning. He took a few practice swings to warm up his muscles while the Cobras warmed up a new pitcher. As he did, he checked the position of the outfielders. None of them had shifted back even a step.

But why would they? he thought. *I walked the only other time at bat this game. They've never seen me hit before. I'm the new kid.*

He moved into the batter's box and hefted the bat.

Well, Cobras, time to get to know me!

CHAPTER FOUR

After Cleanup Day, Carter and Ash biked home together.

"You want to hit the batting cages at the Diamond Champs?" Ash asked. "I'll pay."

The Diamond Champs was an indoor baseball facility that Ash's mother had recently renovated. It boasted brand-new pitching machines in the batting cages, a huge indoor turf field, and well-maintained pitching tunnels. Since its grand opening, Carter had spent a lot of time there—and money.

Carter laughed. "You mean your mom will pay."

"No, I've got money." Ash patted his pocket.

Carter was tempted but shook his head. "Thanks

anyway, but Lucky Boy's been cooped up in the house all day. I want to take him for a long walk before dinner."

Lucky Boy was Carter's black-and-tan dog. He'd earned his name because he'd survived being hit by a car. Carter felt just as lucky, though; he'd rescued the little dog and now had a faithful four-footed companion.

"Going up into the woods?"

Ash's tone was casual, but Carter wasn't fooled. Ash suspected he was hiding something in the forest behind their houses. He was right.

Years ago, Carter and Liam had discovered a natural rock shelter deep in the woods. Almost completely hidden from view from the faint trail that snaked through the woods, it was the perfect hideout. No one but the cousins knew about it—and when he found out the McGraths were moving, Carter had promised Liam to keep it that way.

"Nah," Carter said to Ash. "I never go up there this time of year. Too muddy."

They pedaled in silence for a little ways. Then Ash said, "Hey, Carter, you ever play on a team with a girl before?"

Carter shook his head. "Have you?"

"Yeah. It wasn't good."

"Why not?" Carter asked curiously.

"She was always fussing with her hair. She chased butterflies instead of fly balls. If the ball came at her, she ducked." He shook his head in disgust. "The only thing she could do was hit the ball off the tee and—"

Carter burst out laughing. "Hang on! This was in Tee Ball? Ash, half the kids I played with back then were like that girl. Heck, *I* was like that girl at first!"

"I wasn't." Ash's voice was hard. Carter stopped laughing. "When I played, I played to win. Still do. Don't you?"

Carter chewed on his lower lip. He knew Ash was competitive. He was, too. But sometimes Ash was so intense that he made Carter uncomfortable. Like now.

The boys pulled onto their road a few minutes later. Ash waved good-bye and continued on to his house a short distance away. Carter stashed his bike in the garage and hurried into his kitchen for a snack. Lucky Boy came hurtling down the hall toward him.

"One sec, boy," Carter said, laughing. He made a peanut butter and jelly sandwich, scrawled a note for his parents, and then clipped Lucky Boy's leash to his collar. "Walk time!"

Half an hour and several fire hydrants later, they returned home to the smell of sautéed garlic and other delicious odors. Carter's mother, her brown hair whisked up in a messy bun, was preparing supper in the kitchen.

"Mmm, chicken and veggies," Carter said appreciatively, lifting a lid to peek at the meal. "Is there rice, too, and when do we eat?"

"Yes and soon," she assured him. "Now scoot."

Knowing "soon" usually meant ten minutes, Carter decided to do a little research. He went to his room, fired up his laptop, and typed *knuckleball* into his Internet search engine.

A long list of websites popped up immediately. Carter chose one that offered advice on throwing the pitch.

The website suggested starting with the thumb and pinky gripping the ball. The three other fingers curled in so their tips dug into the surface. Carter grabbed a baseball off his shelf. A southpaw, he held it in his left hand and moved his fingers into the grip as described.

That seems easy enough, he thought. He checked a few other websites, experimenting with holding the ball at the laces and at the smooth part. He read with interest that some people said that throwing the knuckleball hard made it less effective and that of all the pitches, it was one of the trickiest for a catcher to handle.

Good thing Ash will be coming to the pitching clinic, he thought.

The best thing about the knuckleball, or floater, as it was sometimes called, was its bizarre motion. One site said the ball looked as if it were floating as it flew toward the plate.

That should make things interesting for batters, he thought with a grin. He wanted to try it out immediately. But he knew better. *If I'm going to learn it, I've got to convince Mr. Delaney to teach it to me!*

CHAPTER

Liam gripped the handle of the bat tightly and then took a deep breath and relaxed. He had decided to see what the new Cobras hurler had in his arsenal before he swung. So he let the first pitch, a fastball that didn't look all that fast, go by.

"Strike one!"

The next pitch looked as if it were going to fly wide. Liam chose not to swing at that one, either, certain that it was a ball.

"Strike two!" the umpire cried.

Liam frowned slightly at the call, but he didn't argue. He wanted the umpire on his side, after all.

"That's right! Just wait for one you think you can hit!" someone from the stands shouted.

Liam stepped out of the box and looked toward the bleachers. Phillip was staring right at him, arms crossed and a knowing smile on his face. Had he been the one to yell? Liam didn't know for sure.

Who else could it have been, though? he thought.

He knocked the dirt from his cleats, hefted the bat, and got back into his stance.

The third pitch was just like the first two. This time, he swung. *Pow!* The ball flew into the gap between center and right field. As the outfielders scrambled to pick it up, Liam sprinted to first.

"Keep going!" the first-base coach yelled, wheeling his arm frantically.

Liam didn't hesitate. He raced on to second, touched that bag with a firm step, too, and then, with a burst of speed, beat the throw to third. That's where he stopped, breathing hard and smiling.

"Whoa, nice blast, man!"

Liam grinned over his shoulder. Spencer was now the third-base coach, having been replaced by Scott Hoffmann on the mound.

"Thanks," Liam replied.

"I didn't know you could hit like that," Spencer continued. "I thought—"

Whatever else Spencer was about to say was cut off by the sharp crack of a bat. Sean had rapped out a low fly ball just inside the right field foul line.

The Cobras right fielder raced over, glove outstretched. Liam tensed, waiting to see if he made the catch. If the ball landed in the outfielder's glove, then he would stay put at third and hope that Jay Mendoza could hit him home.

The Cobra dove under the ball in time. Sean was out. Liam started to relax when—

"Go, Liam! Go!" Spencer screamed.

Liam didn't think; he just took off like a bullet shot from a gun. Arms pumping, legs churning, he sprinted toward home as fast as he could. Midway there, he glanced up.

The Cobras catcher was on his feet, expecting a play at the plate. Liam steeled himself for a slide. But before he even could think about hitting the dirt—*thud!* The ball landed inside the catcher's mitt!

Liam screeched to a halt and reversed direction back to third.

Thud! The catcher hurled the ball to the third

baseman. The third baseman advanced toward Liam, who quickly backpedaled. *Thud!* The ball flew back to the catcher. Liam was caught in a rundown!

Every Python was on his feet now, yelling instructions. Liam blocked them out. All that mattered was reaching base safely. Third, home, he didn't care which!

The catcher and third baseman quickly closed in. Adrenaline raced through Liam's veins. Breathing hard, he darted back and forth, staying just out of reach. Then suddenly, the catcher, ball in glove, lunged at him. Liam whirled out of the way. With a desperate twist, he tried to skirt around the third baseman to the bag.

He might have made it, too, if he hadn't lost his footing. Instead of sailing to the base, he landed in the dirt just as the catcher tossed the ball to his teammate. *Whap!* The third baseman's glove smacked him in the side.

"Yer out!" the umpire cried.

The Pythons groaned as one. Liam pushed himself to his feet, stood, and dusted off his uniform. As he moved toward the dugout, he glanced at the bleachers.

To get on the All-Star team, he had to earn votes from players, coaches, and members of the Little League board. He'd be going up against more than eighty other players. And that was the problem: He was still the new kid. People didn't know who he was—or worse, knew him as the player who struck out in the World Series.

If I'm going to get enough votes to be an All-Star, I have to do something to stand out from the crowd, something that will erase that World Series whiff from everyone's memories, he thought. *But what?*

CHAPTER SIX

Sunday night at nine o'clock, Carter sat at his desk reading a tattered paperback. Every so often he glanced at his laptop. He was waiting for Liam to get online so they could video-chat. Finally, he heard the alert signal. He put his book aside and tapped a key to accept Liam's call.

A moment later, Liam's image came into focus. Carter noted that his cousin's brown hair was growing out of its crew cut length and that his face had a tan from the California sunshine. Other than that, he was the same old Liam.

"'Bout time, doofus," he grumbled good-naturedly.

"Hey, a guy's gotta eat!" Liam made a face. "Mom

tried to hide spinach in the lasagna again. But I picked it out before I ate any."

"Not all of it," Carter said, "unless that's mold between your front teeth. Seriously, how can you not feel that? It's like a tree between your teeth."

"Hang on." Liam disappeared from the screen. When he returned, he had a long string of dental floss hanging out of his mouth. "Better?" he said with a clownish grin.

"You're a treasure," Carter said dryly. "In fact, someone ought to bury you."

Liam pulled the floss free and tossed it away—in a trash can, Carter sincerely hoped, but just as sincerely doubted. He'd been in Liam's old bedroom enough times to know better.

Carter filled him in on Cleanup Day and the new pitch he hoped to learn. "Oh, and we got a new teammate named Rachel, who—"

Liam let out a guffaw. "First a guy named Ashley and now another one called Rachel?"

"First of all, he goes by Ash," Carter said, "and second, Rachel is a girl."

"Oh!" Liam looked surprised, then curious. "Any problem with that?"

"Not from me." He didn't add that Ash wasn't too keen about her. He'd learned not to say much to Liam about Ash, actually. Liam had never met the Hawks catcher, but that didn't stop him from being jealous of him. Carter understood why his cousin felt that way— Ash had replaced him on the team and lived in his old house, after all—but he hoped Liam would accept the situation soon. Steering around the subject of Ash made for awkward conversation sometimes.

"Okay then, enough about you. Time to talk about me," Liam said. "I have a question."

Carter tipped back in his chair, one foot resting on his desktop and the other on the floor keeping him balanced. "Shoot."

"Bang. My question is, how do I get people to vote for me at All-Star time if they don't know who I am?"

Before Carter could puzzle out what Liam meant, a newcomer joined the conversation.

"Woof!" Lucky Boy burst into the room and leaped into his lap. Carter nearly flipped over backward in his chair. As he flailed his arms to regain his balance, he knocked his book to the floor.

"Lucky Boy, you made me lose my place." He picked up the book and thumbed through the pages. "Sorry, can you say that again?"

But instead of repeating his question, Liam pointed at the book. "Hey, is that what I think it is?"

Carter flipped the book over so Liam could see the title on the cover. "Yep!"

The book was one of his and Liam's favorites. The story was about a young baseball player who meets a mysterious man only he can see. Soon after that meeting, the boy begins hitting home runs every single time he comes to bat. Fame and glory soon follow. Then the man disappears—and with him, the boy's amazing talent. Yet the boy retains something he didn't have before: confidence.

The tattered volume in Carter's hand had once belonged to Liam's father. Now the boys shared it. Their mothers had offered to buy them each their own new copy, but they preferred to take turns rereading the original. Right now, Liam seemed fascinated by the tattered volume.

"Dude, stop staring at the book," Carter said. "You're creeping me out."

Liam looked up, his eyes shining with excitement. "That's it!"

"What's it?"

"That book's the answer!"

"What was the question?!"

Liam explained. "I'm the new kid in my league, right? People barely know me. So who's going to vote for

34

me at All-Star time? No one. Unless"—he stabbed a finger at the screen—"instead of the new kid, I become the home run kid! Everyone loves home runs. Home runs help win games. They inspire other players, boost morale, give runners who might be left on base the chance to cross home plate. Homers pull in spectators who yell and cheer and that makes players work even harder. And then there's the whole Phillip thing. Can you imagine the look on his face if—no, *when*—I claim the home run title?" He sat back at last, laced his fingers behind his head, and grinned. "The way I see it, it's the perfect solution."

Carter bit his lip. He knew what Liam said about home runs was perfectly true. He also knew that when his cousin set his mind to something, nothing anyone said or did could change it. Sometimes his grand visions turned into reality. Last year, for instance, he'd been sure their All-Star team would make it to Williamsport, and he'd been right. But sometimes his plans didn't work out the way he hoped. Carter had a jagged pink scar on his calf, courtesy of a fall from a homemade zipline Liam had built one summer.

Carter didn't want to put a damper on Liam's enthusiasm for his home run quest, but he saw a huge flaw in his plan.

"How?" he asked.

"How what?"

"How are you going to go from someone who hasn't hit a homer yet this season to someone who's hitting them all the time?"

He thought Liam might get exasperated with him then. But Liam just puffed out his chest and laughed. "Dork, it's me. I'll make it work," he said confidently. "I always do!"

Carter lifted his leg in front of the camera and pointed to the scar on his calf. "Always?"

Liam grinned. "Well, *almost* always."

CHAPTER

SEVEN

Liam was so pumped about his idea that he wanted to practice his hitting right away. So after ending his chat session with Carter, he ran downstairs to find someone to pitch to him.

"Sorry, Liam, but I have to finish this presentation for tomorrow," his father said, peering at him over his reading glasses.

"Well, can you give me an extra twenty bucks so I can go to the batting cages then?"

"Sure."

"Really?" Liam brightened. He hadn't expected his father to agree. Usually, when he asked for money beyond his allowance, there was a catch.

"I'll be happy to give you the money," his father said. "Right after your mother tells me you've done twenty dollars' worth of extra chores."

Liam's face fell. "I should've known," he grumbled.

His mother was out shopping, so he couldn't ask her for money or to pitch to him. That left...

"Tell me why, exactly, I would do this?" his sister, Melanie, asked when he cornered her in the kitchen.

"Because you love your little brother and would do anything for him?"

She flipped her long black hair over her shoulder and looked at him speculatively. "Yeah, that's not it."

Liam handed her a bag of Wiffle balls and guided her out the door to the backyard. "Because after we're done here, I'll help you learn your lines for your audition."

Sixteen-year-old Melanie was an aspiring actress. She loved acting, singing, and dancing as much as Liam loved hitting, catching, and running. Moving to California, movie capital of the world, had been her dream come true. Her parents supported that dream and had allowed her to enroll in a private high school that focused on the arts.

Liam's new school was private, too. Much as he hated wearing the school uniform—what boy actually likes wearing a tie?—he was grateful to have ended up there, because Rodney and Sean went to the same school.

Liam had first met the Driscoll brothers at the Little League tryouts. They had introduced themselves as twins. Liam had stared in amazement, for Rodney was a lanky, dark-skinned boy with tight black curls whereas Scan was freckled and fair. After a big laugh, they told Liam the truth: They were both adopted, and by some freak coincidence, they shared the exact same birthday.

Liam had liked them from the start. He liked them even more when he discovered they knew about his history with Phillip DiMaggio but had chosen to treat it as just that: history.

"We were foster kids before Dad adopted us," they revealed once. "He gave us a fresh start. We figure everyone should get one if they want."

Liam thought if he could get his sister to help him, he'd be one step closer to his own fresh start. But Melanie hadn't agreed to his trade-off yet.

"And after you help me with my lines?" she prodded.

He groaned. "I'll partner with you so you can learn that stupid dance routine. Satisfied?"

"Very." She quickly braided her hair into a long rope down her back. "Now, what do I have to do?"

Liam positioned her in a worn-out spot on the grass. "Stand here. Throw the ball there." He pointed to the strike zone outline of the pitch back he'd set up a short distance away. "I'm going to hit it and—"

"Hang on! I'll be standing right here and you're going to hit the ball at me?!"

Liam rolled his eyes. "It's a Wiffle ball! It might sting if it hits you, but that's it."

"Still..." Melanie disappeared into the garage. When she returned, she was wearing Liam's catcher's mask.

"How do you see through this thing?" She staggered like a zombie. "Or stand the smell? It's like I'm locked in a cage with a jar of boy-stink."

Finally, she returned to her spot. "Ready?"

Liam picked up his bat and got into his stance. "Ready."

She threw the first pitch—underhand.

"Melanie, come on. Quit kidding around! This is important to me!"

"What's the big deal, anyway?" she asked, pushing the mask off her face. "Why the need to practice hitting all of a sudden?"

Liam twirled his bat, considering his answer. "When you audition, you do your best to impress the director so you'll get the role you want, right?"

She nodded.

"Well, I'm trying to impress the people who choose the All-Star team."

"By making hits?"

"By making home runs. More than anyone else, hopefully."

Melanie gave a low whistle. "That's a pretty lofty goal, little brother."

"So's trying to be a big-time actress," he shot back.

She held up her hands. "Hey, I didn't say it wasn't possible! But let me pass along some advice from my drama coaches: As you climb the ladder, be careful where you step."

Liam screwed up his face. "That sounds like something out of a fortune cookie. What does it even mean?"

"Think it over. You'll get it. And when you do, keep it in mind, okay?" She replaced the mask and picked up another Wiffle ball. "Ready?"

Liam nodded. This time, the pitch came in overhand and right on target. Liam swung. *Whack!*

The plastic sphere flew high and long, the air whistling through its holes, before coming to a rest on the grass far behind Melanie.

"Not bad, bro," she said with grudging admiration. "Let's see what you can do with this one!"

Liam watched with amusement, and then amazement, as she went into a near-perfect windup. Then she reared back, lunged forward, and threw, snapping her wrist just as she released the ball. Liam was so surprised that he almost didn't swing.

Whack!

The second ball whizzed into the sky and joined the first in the grass.

"How'd you learn to pitch like that?" he asked, still dumbfounded.

She looked offended. "I'm an actress, remember? I transform myself into whatever role I'm given. Right now, I'm playing the role of pitcher." Then she laughed. "Plus, I've been watching Carter pitch for years. I'm just imitating what I saw him do in our yard back home. Only right-handed, of course."

Liam laughed, too.

It was only later, after he'd spent a torturous hour helping her with her lines and stepping on her toes while dancing, that he realized what his starstruck sister had said: *back home.*

Well, what do you know? he thought. *Maybe she misses Pennsylvania, too.*

CHAPTER

Whoa," Carter breathed. "Check out all the flags for baseball."

He and Rachel stood in the entrance to the high school gymnasium. Dozens of championship banners for various sports teams hung from the walls. The baseball banners outnumbered them all.

"Impressive, isn't it?" a gruff voice behind them said. "My son pitched for the team that won three in a row."

Carter and Rachel turned to find a very tall man with piercing black eyes staring down at them. His sharp features reminded Carter of a hawk.

"I'm Mark Delaney," the man said. "And you are...?"

"Rachel Warburton," Rachel replied with a grin,

"and this is Carter Jones, who I predict will help add even more baseball banners when he's in high school!"

"Rachel!" A deep red flush of embarrassment crept up Carter's neck.

Mr. Delaney chuckled. "Carter Jones, yes, your coach told me about you. You too, Rachel. Now go warm up. We're about to start."

As he moved to an open spot on the gleaming hardwood floor, Carter counted ten other players. Three of them, including Ash, were in catcher's gear.

"Hey, Ash!" he called.

Ash waved and started toward him.

"Carter! You ready?" Rachel called.

At the sound of her voice, Ash frowned. Then his arm dropped and he turned back toward the other catchers.

Come on, man, Carter wanted to say, *at least give her a chance.*

The clinic moved briskly from light warm-ups to harder throws to basic pitches. Mr. Delaney and his two assistants, clipboards in hand, assessed the players' mechanics.

Rachel was in line ahead of Carter. He could tell she was nervous by the way she shifted back and forth. "Hey, don't sweat it," he whispered. "Just do what you can."

She shot him a grateful look and then stepped to the practice rubber for her turn. She cupped the ball in her right hand, eyed Ash behind the plate, reared back, and threw.

"Look out!"

The ball flew wild and hit the bleachers with a deafening bang. "Sorry! Sorry!" she cried. Ash shook his head. Even though Carter couldn't see his face, he was sure the catcher was grimacing with disgust.

Now he stepped up for his turn. His mouth was suddenly dry. He swallowed hard.

"Two-seam fastball, when you're ready," Mr. Delaney called.

Carter rotated the baseball to the two-seam grip. Ash held up his glove and gave a slight nod. Eyes focused on his target, Carter went into his windup. Left foot against the rubber, right shoulder aimed at the plate, he raised his right knee and with a great lunging step hurled the ball with all his might.

Thud!

The ball smacked into the mitt. Ash smiled at Carter from behind his mask.

Carter grinned back and then looked at Mr. Delaney. The coach beckoned him over.

"You're hooking your wrist," he informed Carter.

He demonstrated the problem. Ball in hand, he held his arm outstretched behind his back and flexed his wrist so his palm faced down. "See that bend? Straighten it out. You'll have more control because you'll have less movement through your wrist when you throw. Got it?"

Carter nodded. The next time he threw, Mr. Delaney said, "Better. But keep working on it."

The clinic ended after an hour. One by one, people gathered their belongings and left. Rachel waved to Carter before heading out the door. Now only Carter, Ash, and the coaches remained.

Carter's stomach sank. Mr. Delaney had said nothing to him about the knuckleball. Trying to hide his disappointment, he slung his bag over his shoulder.

"Better put that down, Carter," Mr. Delaney said. "It'll just get in your way when you throw."

"Throw?"

The coach smiled. "You do want to work on the knuckleball, don't you?"

"Yes, sir!" Carter dropped his bag and picked up a ball. "I think I already know the grip." He imagined the photos he'd seen online and showed Mr. Delaney how he was holding the ball.

The coach made a slight adjustment to his thumb

position. "You throw it just like a regular fastball but without as much force. If thrown correctly, it will bobble the whole way down."

"And confuse the batter!"

"Exactly," Mr. Delaney said. "Now, without letting go of the ball, show me how you'd throw it."

Carter pantomimed the pitch in slow motion. "Like that?"

"Good."

Mr. Delaney asked Ash to get back behind the plate. Then he spread his hands wide. "Well? What are you waiting for? Let's see your knuckleball, Carter!"

Carter didn't need a second invitation. Eyeballing the pocket of Ash's glove, he double-checked his grip, using his sense of touch rather than sight to make minor tweaks. Then he took a deep breath, wound up, and threw.

Thud! The ball socked into Ash's glove. Carter thought it had jumped just a little, but he wasn't sure. When he looked at Mr. Delaney, though, he knew he'd done it right. The tall man was smiling broadly.

"Carter," he said, "you are what we call a natural." His dark eyes drifted to the banners. "You remind me of my son, actually."

For a moment, Carter thought he saw a shadow of sadness pass over the coach's face. But if so, it was gone the next moment.

"Of course," the coach said, eyes back on Carter, "that first pitch may have been beginner's luck! Ready to throw a few more before we call it a night?"

Carter grinned. "Absolutely!"

CHAPTER NINE

I'm starving," Sean said. "Rodney, are there any cookies left?"

It was Tuesday afternoon. Liam and the Driscolls had just arrived at the ball field for their game against the Vipers.

"Let me see." Rodney opened a snack bag and pulled out a big chocolate-chip cookie. "Last one, but it's mine because—hey!"

With lightning speed, Sean had swiped the cookie out of his brother's hand. Now, slowly and deliberately, he licked the bottom. "Oh, sorry, did you want this?" He held the cookie out to Rodney.

"Gross!"

"Boys," Dr. Driscoll said. "Please save your energy for the game. And your disgusting jokes for when we're not in public."

Laughing, the boys hustled onto the grassy field to warm up. Liam was slated to start in center field, but he didn't mind. Today, he planned to focus on what he did at the plate rather than behind it.

The Pythons were the visiting team and so had first raps. As usual, Reggie led off. Liam, batting sixth this game instead of seventh, leaned forward, eyes on the boy on the mound.

"Enrique Herrera. Age twelve. Throws righty, bats righty," he murmured.

"Liam McGrath. Age twelve. Talks to himself," Sean murmured in exact imitation of Liam.

"Quiet," Liam growled good-naturedly. "I'm trying to remember what I know about this pitcher." In preparation for the day's game, he had studied the Vipers pitcher's stats and pored over past Vipers games.

"Oh. So what else do you know about him?"

"He's struck out ten batters in fifteen innings played so far this season. Also given up two home runs."

He almost added, *Soon to be three, if I get a pitch I like.*

But he kept quiet. He hadn't told anyone except

50

Melanie and Carter about his quest for the home run title. He wanted to have some big hits under his belt first. Otherwise, it would look like empty bragging.

And, a little voice inside his head whispered, *you won't look foolish if you fail.*

He pushed the voice aside and watched the Viper throw.

Fastball low and outside. Reggie let it go by. He knocked the second down for a grounder. It was an easy pickup and an even easier out.

"Nice try, man," Liam said when Reggie returned to the bench.

Alex popped out, bringing up Robert. Robert took a vicious cut at the first pitch. The ball might have sailed far if he'd hit it cleanly. But he fouled for strike one. Three swings later, he struck out.

Luckily, Scott did just as good a job on the mound for the Pythons. The teams switched sides with goose eggs on both sides of the board.

"Things keep going like this, and we'll have a really quick game," Sean commented.

"Guess I better do something to slow things down then," Rodney said. He selected his bat, put on his helmet—and then hit six fouls in a row.

He's throwing fastballs low and outside, Liam wanted to scream. Rodney must have recognized that, too, for he laced the seventh pitch for a single.

"All right!" the Pythons cried.

Devon Shute, up second that inning, muffed a bunt attempt. He got the signal to swing away. Like Rodney, he clipped the ball for several fouls. Unlike Rodney, he struck out.

Now Liam approached the plate. He glanced at Dr. Driscoll and got the signal to bunt.

Liam bit his lip in disappointment. But when the pitch came, he squared off and laid down a sacrifice good enough to get Rodney to second. Liam was thrown out at first.

I hope it was worth it, he thought. But Rodney was left on base when Clint flied out.

As he jogged to center field, Liam glanced at the scoreboard. *Next time,* he thought. *Next time, I'll blast it out of the park and get a run up there!*

But when he came to the plate again in the fourth inning, it was the same situation as before: runner on first, one out.

Great, Liam thought as he got up from the bench. *Just great. I'll be told to do another bunt.*

Then something crossed his mind. He pushed it

away and selected a bat. But as he started walking to the plate, the thought came rushing back.

If I don't look at the coach...

Heart pounding, he fiddled with his helmet, adjusted his batting glove, and stepped into the box. He kept his eyes glued to the pitcher. Not once did he glance at Dr. Driscoll.

The pitch came. He swung. Bat hit ball and—*pow!*

"Holy cow!" he heard someone yell.

Home run! As he rounded the bases, Liam felt like shouting for joy.

Sean was the first to meet him at the plate. "Mighty impressive, my man!" The other Pythons slapped him on the back and congratulated him, too.

In the dugout, Dr. Driscoll called him aside. "Not that I'm complaining about a two-run homer," the coach said, his expression bemused, "but why did you swing away? I was giving you the sign to bunt."

Liam's heart skipped a beat. "You—you were? Oh. I guess I didn't see it."

Technically, it wasn't a lie—he hadn't seen the sign. But deep down, he knew he was in the wrong.

Then he looked at the scoreboard. *Two runs thanks to me. Maybe I was in the wrong, but it turned out all right!*

CHAPTER TEN

The Saturday morning after the pitching clinic, the Hawks met in the center of town to march with the other local Little League teams in the Opening Day parade. It was a glorious spring day, bright and clear and warm. Players from all the baseball divisions, from the littlest kids in Tee Ball to the teenagers in the Juniors, Seniors, and Big League, were grouped at the end of the line. The Little League Softball teams crowded together in the middle, their players chatting excitedly.

At the front of the line was the town's newest squad representing the Little League Challenger Division. As its name implied, this group was made up of players with physical and mental disabilities. None of those challenges stopped them from playing baseball, however.

"Is everybody here?" Coach Harrison called. It was hard to hear him over the din of the crowd lining the sidewalks and the sounds of the high school marching band members tuning their instruments.

"Rachel's missing," Carter answered.

"Guess we'll have to march without her," Ash said.

"Then again, maybe you won't!" Rachel bounded up, breathless. "Sorry I'm late, Coach. I was talking to Mr. Delaney."

Carter looked at her with surprise. "I didn't know he was going to be here."

"Me neither," she said. "I just ran into him up in the front of the line. Did you know his son is—?"

Whatever she was about to say was cut off by the crash of cymbals followed by the thrum of drumbeats. Applause rose from the spectators. Rachel added to the noise, clapping and chanting at the top of her lungs.

"Here we go, Haw-awks. Here we go!"

The rest of the team took up the cheer. Other baseball squads countered with cries of their own.

"Eagles! One-two-three! Eagles! One-two-three!"

"Raptors rule! Raptors rule!"

"Go, Falcons, go! Go, Falcons, go!"

"Chickadees! Chickadees! Rah, rah, rah!" a choir of tiny voices warbled.

Ash made a face. "Chickadees?"

"Tee Ball team," Carter explained. "The league's Board of Directors assigned bird names to the different divisions years ago. They thought birds of prey weren't right for the little kids."

"What were you back then?"

Carter laughed. "Liam and I were Canaries. But it was better than Hummingbirds!"

After the parade, the Hawks met up at the field to have their team picture taken. Then it was time to prepare for their first game of the season. Many spectators were there already, including Carter's parents.

"Smile, Carter!" Mrs. Jones called. Before he could stop her, she took his photo.

His mother had taken snapshots at every Opening Day. She had framed each one and hung them in order, from Canary to last year's Hawk, in the front hallway of their house.

Carter wished she had skipped the picture this year. In all the others, he and Liam stood with their arms around each other's shoulders, big toothy grins on their faces. In this photo, he was alone.

"Hey, how about a shot with his favorite teammate?"

Rachel appeared out of nowhere. She twisted her baseball cap to one side, jammed her hands under her armpits, and scowled at the camera. "How's this? Pretty intimidating, huh? Bet those Eagles are going to be shaking in their cleats today when they get a load of me."

In the past week, Carter had discovered something about Rachel: She reminded him of Liam. For one thing, she knew as many stupid jokes as his cousin did. For another, she could throw with almost as much power. Her cannon of an arm had earned her the respect of her teammates—or most of them, anyway.

"I thought it was going to be weird having a girl on the team," second baseman Kevin Pinto confessed midweek. "But it isn't."

"Oh, yeah. It's just great," Ash muttered under his breath.

Carter saw Rachel's eyes flick to Ash. If she had heard his comment, though, she didn't let on. Carter wondered if it was because she didn't want to make waves. If so, then he decided he wouldn't, either—although he thought Ash was out of line.

Now Carter saw the catcher waving to him frantically.

"We need to go over the signals again," Ash said, his voice urgent.

Carter's stomach tightened. Ash had been pushing him all week long to focus more and try harder. He wanted to tell Ash to ease up. Instead, he ran through the signals.

"One finger means changeup. Two means two-seam fastball. Three means four-seam fastball. You'll flash four signals in a row. The third one is the pitch I throw."

"Okay, good," Ash said. He reached behind him and pulled a thick blue binder out of his gear bag. He thumbed to a page marked *Eagles*. "I've seen some of these guys at the Diamond Champs batting cages. This guy Craig"—he tapped a name on a chart—"has been there a lot. So watch out for him. And this other guy—"

"Ash, don't worry. I'll be careful!"

The catcher held up a cautionary finger, his dark brown eyes boring into Carter's. "Just. Be. Ready."

Half an hour later, the game against the Eagles began. Carter soon discovered that Ash was right: The Eagles did have some powerful bats. In the first inning, they made those bats talk.

Ash was talking, too. "Come on, come on, come on. Here you go, Jones, here you go, here you go, here you go!"

Carter knew Ash thought a steady stream of chatter helped motivate pitchers. But it plucked at Carter's nerves like fingers on guitar strings. His pitching suffered, and the Eagles racked up three runs in the first inning before the Hawks retired the side. In the dugout, the knot of anxiety in Carter's stomach was tighter than ever.

Then Rachel sat down beside him. "Hey, Carter, did I ever tell you about my first at bat?"

"No," he muttered.

"I couldn't figure out why the baseball was getting bigger. And then it hit me."

Carter waited for her to tell him what she'd figured out. Then, he got it.

"It hit you," he repeated, a small smile curving on his lips. "Yet another lame joke."

"Know why I don't play softball?" She leaned in closer. "It's an underhanded sport."

Carter's smile grew.

"Know how I ended up in my position on the Hawks defense?" she continued, her blue eyes snapping with glee. "I followed a piece of advice: If at first you don't succeed"—she paused for comic effect—"try outfield!"

Carter started laughing—and all at once, the knot in his stomach loosened.

"Thanks, Rach," he said. "I needed that."

Rachel glanced at Ash. The catcher had just made the last out of the inning. A scowl etched his face as he pulled on his pads. When he saw them sitting together, his scowl deepened.

"Yeah, I know you did," Rachel said. "Now grab your glove and hit the mound. And Jones? Relax out there. Baseball's supposed to be fun."

CHAPTER

ELEVEN

Liam paced back and forth in front of the bench, slapping his glove against his leg with each step. The game against the Sidewinders was about to begin, and he couldn't sit still.

"Liam, will you stop?" Rodney admonished. "You're using up all your energy in here."

"Can I help it if I'm pumped?" Liam replied.

"Pumped enough to hit another homer today?" Spencer asked.

Since his four-bagger against the Vipers, Liam had hit one other homer, a walk-off in the Pythons' first meeting with the Anacondas. Unlike his first home run, the second left him guilt-free.

It also inched him up a notch on the league's home run leaderboard. The name just above his was Phillip DiMaggio. If he homered today, he and Phillip would be tied with three apiece. And if he jumped ahead of Phillip at some point? That would be sweet—and would, he was sure, earn him some All-Star votes.

"Gonna try for two," he said in reply to Spencer's question.

"That'd be great," Sean said, "but for now—sit down! You're wearing a groove in the dirt."

Liam moved to the open spot next to Spencer and pointed a finger at the pitcher. "Speaking of grooves, we're going to find ours out there today, right?"

"Find it? I didn't realize it was lost!"

"Well, just in case..." Liam cupped his hands around his mouth. "Groove! Groove? Hey, anybody seen our groove?"

Cracking up, Spencer and the Driscolls began to imitate him. "Yoo-hoo, groove? We're missing a groove here!"

The other Pythons looked at them as if they were crazy, which just made them laugh harder. Then the umpire called, "Play ball!" and they settled down to business.

The Pythons and Sidewinders hadn't faced each other yet. But the night before, Liam had read through every one of the Sidewinders game recaps, noting the names of their strongest batters. He shared his information with Coach Driscoll and Spencer.

The coach nodded approvingly. "Been doing your homework, I see. Good. A catcher who knows his opponents is a big help."

"Watch out for Kyle Flanders, their cleanup batter," Liam reminded the pitcher as they jogged onto the field for the first inning, "and their center fielder, Matt Finch. He's sixth in the lineup and hit a homer his last game. We don't want him adding another this game."

The first inning went by scoreless for both teams. Kyle started off the second. A muscular boy with a mean glint in his eye, he looked like a typical bully to Liam.

To Spencer, he must have looked even worse—the pitcher's expression reminded Liam of a deer caught in car headlights.

Hold it together, Spence, Liam willed silently. He pounded his glove to get his attention. Spencer blinked and then nodded. Liam flashed the signal for a pitch low and outside. Spencer nodded again, wound up, and threw.

The pitch sailed high and inside. The Sidewinder jumped back with a yelp.

"Ball!" the umpire called.

"No kidding," the Sidewinder muttered.

The next two pitches also flew wild. Liam called for time.

"Spencer, calm down. You're letting him get to you."

"I know," the pitcher said miserably. "It's just—I can feel him staring at me."

Liam pointed to the center of his mitt. "Focus all your attention here, then. Okay?"

Spencer heaved a sigh. "I'll try."

Hoping to get Spencer to crack a smile, Liam quoted one of his and Carter's favorite movie lines. "No, not try. 'Do or do not. There is no try.'"

Instead of a smile, Spencer's face wrinkled in confusion. "Huh?"

"Jedi Master Yoda?" When Spencer's expression didn't change, Liam shook his head and told the pitcher to forget it.

So much for that groove, he thought as he hustled back to the plate.

Spencer's fourth pitch was more in control but, unfortunately, still outside the zone.

"Take your base," the umpire instructed the batter.

The Sidewinder tossed the bat aside and jogged down the path, grinning.

Go ahead, Liam thought. *Smile now. Because you won't be smiling later. I guarantee it.*

CHAPTER
TWELVE

Wonder if Liam's heard those lame-o jokes before? Carter thought as he hurried to the mound. As he jabbed his foot into the ground by the rubber, he made a mental note to repeat Rachel's "groaners" the next time they talked. He knew his cousin would appreciate the humor. He did, too, if only because they made him feel looser than he had the first inning.

The Eagles had lit him up like a pinball machine then. After that success, the first batter came to the plate with a swagger and a smile.

Bet he thinks I'm going to dish up more meatballs, Carter thought. *Well, I hope he likes 'em with extra mustard, 'cause that's what I'm serving now!*

Three screaming fastballs and a tricky changeup later, the Eagle slunk back to his bench with his wings clipped.

"Here we go!" Ash cried. He threw the ball to Leonard Frick at third, who sent it to Kevin at second. Kevin fired it to Miguel Martinez. Carter held out his glove. Miguel threw, and the ball hit the pocket with a satisfying thud.

The next Eagle was a familiar face. Craig Ruckel had been on the All-Star team with Carter and Liam the year before. He'd been an inconsistent batter then. But the practice in the Diamond Champs batting cages paid off, because he creamed Carter's first pitch. It was a line drive that rocketed toward the gap between Kevin and Miguel.

Or would have, if a right-handed pitcher had been on the mound. But Carter was a lefty; he wore his glove on his right hand. With a quick sideways leap off the hill, he nabbed the ball out of the air for out number two. Craig, midway down the base path, slowed his step and then veered back to his bench, shaking his head all the way.

"One more, Hawks. One more!" Rachel cried from right field.

Carter cradled the ball, waiting for Ash's signals. But when they came—two fingers, then one, then four, then one again—he blinked in confusion.

The third signal marked the pitch. But what Ash had shown didn't make sense. One finger was a changeup. Two was a two-seam fastball. Three was a four-seam fastball. Was four . . . *the knuckleball?*

Carter immediately shook off Ash. He'd had one more pitching session with Mr. Delaney and Ash, but no way was his knuckleball ready. He hadn't even shown it to Coach Harrison yet.

Something struck him then. Ash received the signals from Coach Harrison and then gave them to Carter. Coach Harrison wouldn't have shown four fingers.

Is Ash trying to call the game himself? he wondered.

Ash shifted in his crouch and flashed another set of signals: Two, one, two, three, followed by a tap to his thigh. Two-seam to the inside. Carter nodded, wound up, and threw.

The ball flew close to the batter's waist. He jumped back out of the way.

"Ball one!"

Carter would have liked a strike, but the pitch had had one thing in its favor. When the Eagle got back into his stance, he stood a few inches farther back from the plate. Not that his new position helped him. He struck out swinging.

"Woo-hoo!" Rachel cheered when she returned to the dugout. "Nice heat, Jones!"

"Thanks," Carter said. "Hey, Ash, you look thirsty. Come get a drink with me."

When they were alone by the water jug, Carter turned and said meaningfully, "Nice calls out there."

Ash furrowed his brow. "What are you talking about?"

"Come on, Ash," Carter chided. "You gave a four-finger signal. You wanted me to throw the knuckleball."

Ash's face darkened. "First of all, I don't call the pitches. Coach Harrison does. Second, I didn't show four fingers. And third," he lowered his voice, "keep it down about that pitch, will you?"

"Why?" Carter waved an arm at his teammates. "They're going to see it soon enough. What's the big deal if they hear about it first?"

"Hear about what?" Rachel appeared next to Carter, empty water cup in hand. "What are you guys talking about?"

Ash gave him a warning look.

Carter ignored him. "Mr. Delaney is teaching me this new pitch." He quickly told her about the knuckleball. "If I can get it to work, it could be really good."

"It would have been devastating," Ash said, "if you hadn't opened your mouth."

Carter turned to him. "What is the big deal?" he asked again, exasperated.

But it was Rachel who answered. "The more people who know you're learning the pitch, the less effective it could be, because they'll be on guard."

"Exactly," Ash said.

She nodded thoughtfully. "Listen, Carter, Ash. I promise I won't say a word to anyone about this. The... *you-know-what*...will be our secret. Well, until it's thrown during a game, anyway. After that, I'm guessing everyone will be talking about it. But until then, not a word. Okay?"

For the second time in less than a minute, Ash agreed with her. Carter decided that if sharing a secret was what it took to make them get along, he was all for it.

"Works for me," he said.

CHAPTER
THIRTEEN

The Sidewinders cleanup batter didn't stay on first base for long. His teammate clocked a hopping ground ball a few feet away from second. Sean darted sideways off the bag, made a clean pickup, and flipped the ball to Clint. Kyle was out. Clint immediately relayed the ball to Reggie. Reggie stretched, toe on first, and caught it a split second before the runner reached the base.

"Yes!" Coach Driscoll called. "Well done!"

The double play must have boosted Spencer's confidence because he mowed down the center fielder to end the inning.

"Good effort," the coach praised. "Now let's get some runs on our side of the board!"

"I'm on it, Coach Dad," Rodney said, earning laughs from his teammates. Then he earned applause with a powerful single to shallow left field.

Liam was up next. When the pitch came, the ball looked as big as a volleyball to him. *Pow!* His teammates jumped to their feet, clapping madly.

"Yes!" he shouted. "Two on the board!"

And home run number three, he added silently. *Take that, DiMaggio, and take notice, All-Star folks!*

"Beautiful blast, man!" Sean enthused. "If we'd caught it on video, it'd be top of the sports highlight reel!"

Liam grinned. "Maybe I should get my sister here to record our games. Then we could watch my—I mean, *our*—highlights anytime we wanted."

He'd said it as a joke. But it suddenly struck him that it wasn't a bad idea. And if he posted the videos online, Carter could see his games firsthand.

Other people, too, he thought with growing excitement. *Like the All-Star voters. Or scouts!*

He let himself imagine it: A scout looking for fresh talent watching his highlight reel, then picking up the phone to ask who the wonder boy was . . .

Talk about a fantasy! But even as he shook his head at his crazy dream, he made a mental note to invite Melanie to the next game. If she wouldn't come, then maybe her video camera would!

Those two runs were the only ones the Pythons got that inning. Neither team scored in the third.

"Only three innings away from our first shutout," Liam noted to Spencer on the bench. "We'll do our part to keep 'em scoreless. But you're the key. The play starts with you. One easy pitch to the wrong batter"—he slapped his palms together and then flew one hand high into the air—"and it's good-bye ball!"

Spencer squirmed. "No pressure, though," he muttered.

Something in the pitcher's voice set off warning bells in Liam's head. "Hey, if you can't handle it, tell the coach so he can replace you before it's too late."

"I can handle it," Spencer said. But he didn't sound sure—and the bells got louder.

"Seriously, man, I—I mean, we—can't afford to give up a run. Our offense isn't exactly racking 'em up, and I can only hit so many homers in one game, you know."

He'd meant it as a joke, but the look on Spencer's face told him it hadn't sounded that way. When he saw that look reflected in the faces of other teammates, too, he reddened.

"Liam, you're up," the coach called.

Relieved, he jumped off the bench.

"Go get 'em," Sean said. No one else added anything more. Liam felt about one inch tall.

Maybe I'll get another homer, he thought hopefully.

He came close with a blast that soared toward the center-field fence. He was disappointed when it was caught for the inning's last out—until he realized the Sidewinder made the catch because he'd backed up when Liam came to the plate.

They're getting scared of my bat, he thought gleefully as he suited up in his gear. *Wonder where they'll stand next time I'm up—the grass behind the fence?*

He was still thinking about his next at bat as he took his position behind the plate and settled into his crouch. That's why he didn't notice who the batter was until— *crack!*

Matt Finch smashed the ball to the exact same spot where Liam's had flown. There was just one difference: Robert wasn't far enough back to make the catch. Home run, Sidewinders.

Liam called for time.

"I warned you about him," he rebuked Spencer. "So much for the shutout." *And so much for keeping Finch to a single homer on the leaderboard,* he thought.

The Pythons pitcher stabbed his toe into the ground. "I'm sorry."

Liam let out a frustrated sigh and turned away. "Yeah, well, so am I."

"Did you warn the outfielders, too?"

Liam froze. "Did I—what?"

"Warn the outfielders," Spencer repeated. "You know, tell them to back up when he was hitting."

Liam's heart sank. He hadn't warned them.

The home run wasn't Spencer's fault. It was his.

CHAPTER FOURTEEN

"Oh boy, better call nine-one-one," Rachel cried, "because the Hawks offense is on *fire*!"

By the bottom of the third inning, Carter and his teammates had racked up fourteen runs to the Eagles' three. Carter grabbed his glove, preparing to head to the field for the top of the fourth. But Mr. Harrison called him back.

"Outstanding job today," he said, "but it's time for you to have a rest and someone else to have a go."

That someone else, it turned out, was Rachel. She'd come out of the game the previous inning and had been throwing to their teammate Seth Wynne during the Hawks' turn at bat.

"Now? Really? I thought I was practicing for later. But now is great!" she said happily.

"Are you replacing me with Seth, Coach?" Ash asked.

"No, you're still in for now," Mr. Harrison replied. "So head to the field and warm her up, please."

"Fine."

Carter had hoped that their agreement about the knuckleball had forged something of a bond between them. But clearly it hadn't, because, unlike Rachel, Ash didn't sound happy. The coach had turned away and didn't hear his tone. But Rachel did.

"Good grief, you would have thought he had to waltz with me," she stage-whispered to Carter.

Carter bit his lip to keep from laughing. Now, as she prepared to face her first batter, he leaned forward, elbows on knees, curious to see how she would do on the mound—and how Ash would do as her catcher.

He hadn't considered what the spectators might do.

"What the heck?" someone said incredulously. "What's a *girl* doing out there?"

Carter looked over his shoulder. The speaker was a teenage boy with a mop of brown hair and a wide gap between his two front teeth. He was standing in the top corner of the bleachers, arms draped over the railing.

"Isn't someone going to tell her she's on the wrong

field?" the teen said, his voice louder. "The softball game's over there!"

Now Carter saw his mother crane her neck, obviously trying to identify the heckler. But she couldn't see him from her seat in the front row.

The umpire straightened and glanced toward the bleachers, too. Carter hoped he was going to ask the teen to leave. But then he realized the official didn't know who had spoken any more than his mother did.

Should I point him out? he wondered. He dismissed the idea as soon as he had it. The teen seemed to be finished, and Carter didn't want to give him an opening to yell again. *I can always describe him to the ump later if I have to.*

The umpire allowed Rachel some practice pitches and then called for the game to resume.

The first Eagle approached the plate. Carter sucked in his breath. Two of the Eagles' three runs had come from an RBI triple hit by this player. In his second at bat, he'd singled. If he got a hold of a pitch he liked—

Crack!

The Hawks on the bench let out a groan. The Eagle had homered off Rachel's first pitch!

"Oh, nice going!"

This time, Carter's mother zeroed in on the source of the heckling. She stood up, hands on hips, and stared at him over the heads of the other people in the crowd. Carter held his breath, waiting for her to confront the boy and dreading the moment she did.

Luckily, the umpire had figured out who'd spoken, too. He waved his arms through the air, indicating that play was to stop, and strode toward the bleachers.

"Yeah, yeah, don't worry, I'm going," the teen said. "I was about to leave anyway. I came here to see my brother play some baseball, not watch some girl blow the Hawks' lead." He banged his way down the bleachers and jutted his chin at someone in the Hawks dugout. "Text me when you're done, Drew."

Carter turned and stared at his teammate Drew Meeker. So did the other Hawks.

Drew scowled. "What are you all looking at me for? I didn't say anything!"

No, Carter thought, *but you didn't tell your brother to shut up, either. That makes you just as bad as him.*

And what about you? a little voice inside his head rebuked. *You could have said something. But you didn't. What does that make you?*

Carter swallowed. *A hypocrite, that's what. A hypocrite and a coward and a lousy teammate.*

"Excuse me, sir?" All eyes turned to the mound. Rachel tossed the ball into the air and caught it. "Can we get back to the game now? Because, for some reason, I'm suddenly all fired up to play."

Laughter and applause rippled through the stands. The umpire smiled, clapped his hands, and cried, "You heard her! Play ball!"

CHAPTER

Liam plucked the last cheese curl from his snack bowl and ate it. Atomic orange cheese dust stained his fingertips. So when his laptop started blooping, he had to wipe them on his shirt before he could answer Carter's video-chat call.

"Is there a doofus in the house?" his cousin asked.

"No, but there's a dork on my screen," Liam replied. "So? How'd Opening Day go?"

Carter gave a thumbs-up. "We won, fourteen to four. I pitched the first three innings and Rachel closed it out in the fourth. The game ended then."

Liam nodded. "Ten-run rule, huh?"

Little League's ten-run rule ended games after four

innings if the visiting team was ahead by ten runs, or after three and a half if the home team was up by that same margin.

"Yep," Carter said, nodding. "How'd your game go?"

Liam hesitated before answering. Then he seesawed his hand in the air. "I got a two-run homer," he said, "but I let the Sidewinders' big hitter get a home run, too." He told Carter about neglecting to tell the outfielders to move back.

Carter frowned. "Dude, that's not like you. You always know what's happening on the field. That's why you're such a great catcher—you see everything and anticipate what might happen next. No one reads a game like you do."

"Stop it, man, you're going to make me blush," Liam said, trying to lighten the mood. He appreciated what Carter said about his catching. But the frown on his cousin's face told him Carter had more to say than compliments. Sure enough—

"It's the whole home run thing, isn't it? You're letting that take up so much space in your brain, it's crowding everything else out. Am I right?"

"No, I—"

"If you had a thought balloon hanging over your head, it'd have one word in it: home run."

"First of all, that's two words and secondly—"

Carter jabbed a finger at him. "Quick, what's the name of the Pythons substitute shortstop?"

Liam blinked in confusion. "What? It's Kevin—no, wait, not Kevin. It's—it's *Devon*." He threw his hands up in frustration. "But what does it matter?"

"It matters," Carter said slowly, "because he's your teammate. He's your teammate and you don't even know his name."

Liam fell silent. "I do know his name, and I know what I'm doing," he said finally. "You don't get it, Carter. I'm the new kid here. If I'm going to make the All Star team this summer, I have to make sure people know who I am. Hitting home runs will do that better than anything else. I'm sure of it."

Carter looked as if he was about to say something else. But instead, he scrubbed his hands over his face and yawned. "Listen, doofus, I should get going. It's three hours later here, and I had a game today, too. I'm beat."

"Yeah, okay. We'll talk again soon. Right?"

" 'Course we will. See ya." And with that, Carter's face disappeared from Liam's screen.

Two afternoons later, the Pythons lost their first game of the season. The defeat came at the hands of the

Copperheads, a good but not great team. Liam hoped to rack up another home run, but the Copperheads made sure he didn't get it. They walked him twice. His third at bat was a long hit that landed in the center fielder's glove.

Next up in their schedule was the Rattlers. With identical records of five wins and one loss, both squads were looking for the upset. Liam was looking for more. He was determined to homer off a pitch thrown by Phillip DiMaggio.

Dark clouds scudded across the sky the day of the game. The umpires and coaches kept looking up and borrowing a spectator's tablet computer to check the weather forecast. A game might be held in drizzle, but the fields would be cleared at the first sound of thunder or flash of lightning.

A storm of a different sort was raging inside Liam. Every time he glimpsed Phillip DiMaggio, that storm threatened to burst forth. But he held himself in check.

Channel your anger into your pitching, he'd once advised Carter. He planned to take his own advice and channel his nervous energy into his hitting. But until the game began, that energy had nowhere to go.

"Dude, quit it, will you?" Sean complained from his seat next to Liam. "You're shaking the whole dugout!"

"Huh?"

Sean looked pointedly at Liam's leg, which was jack-hammering so fast it was more blur than flesh.

"Sorry," Liam said. He stood up and began pacing.

"And now he's doing his caged-lion routine," Rodney commented, "making another groove in the dirt."

"Groove?" Spencer laughed. "Does someone see a groove? Well, keep an eye on it, because Liam and I will need it out there. Right, Liam?"

Liam halted and stared at the pitcher. "We're going to need *focus* out there. Think you've got that today?"

Spencer's laughter died. "Yeah, sure, man," he mumbled.

"Liam," Rodney said quietly.

"What? Oh. Right. Listen, I'm sorry, Spencer. I didn't mean anything by it. I'm just on edge because of—well, you know why."

Spencer gave him a puzzled look. "I do?"

Liam rolled his eyes. "Uh, yeah! Remember?" He jerked his thumb toward the Rattlers dugout.

Spencer glanced over. His eyes widened. He suddenly appeared so nervous that Liam regretted pointing Phillip out to him.

But I had to, he thought. *He's got to be ready for DiMaggio. And so do I.*

CHAPTER
SIXTEEN

After their huge victory against the Eagles, the Hawks hoped to romp over their next opponents, the Raptors. But that game was much closer. Drew was on the mound. Carter watched the first three innings from the bench, and then substituted in for Leonard at third base. Carter saw plenty of action in the "hot corner" that afternoon, and even made a diving catch on a pop foul ball. He got to bat twice, singling the first time and then lining out to the pitcher the second time. He was disappointed not to score either trip to the plate, but in the end the Hawks didn't need a run from him. They squeaked out a 5–4 victory.

Afterward, Coach Harrison called the team together.

"Before I talk about the game, I want to remind everyone that there's still time to volunteer to be a Challenger buddy. It's a great program that pairs players from Little League Baseball and Softball with players in the Challenger Division. Your job would be to help your buddy during their games."

That said, he moved on to a quick critique of the game, pointing out places he thought they could improve and noting specific moments when players gave the extra effort needed to win. When his diving catch was mentioned, Carter blushed with pride.

Next up after the Raptors were the Falcons. The weather that Saturday morning was cool and sunny. Too sunny, actually—Carter's mother insisted he apply sunscreen to his face.

"Mom, I'll be wearing my cap," Carter protested.

"And you'll be wearing sunscreen," she returned, "so you'll be doubly protected." She handed him the tube and left to find a seat.

With an exasperated sigh, he squeezed the lotion onto his fingers and spread it on his cheeks and forehead.

"Is it all rubbed in?" he asked Rachel.

"Oh, most definitely," she replied.

"No, it isn't!" Ash interjected, frowning. "You look like a clown."

"Aw, Ash, you're such a party pooper," Rachel said.

Ash cut her a look but didn't reply.

Carter finished rubbing the lotion onto his cheeks and then hurried to the restroom to wash his hands.

Ash barged in behind him. "Why do you put up with her?" he demanded.

Carter stared at him in the mirror. "Who, Rachel?"

"You don't get it, do you?" Ash paced the concrete floor, his cleats rapping out an angry rhythm. "She could ruin our World Series hopes!"

Carter burst out laughing. "Are you kidding me? How?"

Ash stopped. "Say she starts pitching regularly. Batters who face her could be thrown off because she's a girl. If they're thrown off, they'll hit poorly and she'll earn good stats. If she gets good stats as a girl pitcher, she'll grab headlines. The All-Star selection committee will see those headlines and before you know it, *boom!*"— he smacked his hand on the sink, making Carter jump—"they choose her for the team."

"I still don't see the problem," Carter said. He pushed

the restroom door open, stepped outside, and started walking back toward the dugout. Ash kept pace. "If she can get batters out, then—"

"She might get them out in our league, sure!" Ash said. They had almost reached the dugout, but Ash apparently had more to say, for he grabbed Carter's arm and pulled him back. "But tell me this: How would Rachel do in All-Star competition? She'd be facing players who are at the top of the league, and they only get better the further we advance in the postseason. You know that. You've been there!"

Carter crossed his arms over his chest, thinking back to the previous summer. Ash had a point. The competition had been fierce, from district play to sectional, from state to regional, and onto the World Series. He himself had struggled at times. If it hadn't been for Liam's support, he wasn't sure he would have been able to fight for as long and as hard as he had. He considered Rachel a good player, but did she have that kind of stamina?

Then he shook himself. "Hang on, Ash, we're getting way ahead of ourselves here," he said. "I mean, it's only the third game of the season. All-Star selections aren't for another two months. A lot could happen between now and then."

"Okay, then maybe think about it this way," Ash said. "There are lots of people out there who don't think girls should be playing in Little League Baseball. They'll be watching Rachel, judging her, and talking about everything she does, right or wrong. What if she cracks under that pressure? What kind of chance do we have then to make it to Williamsport?"

Carter chewed on his bottom lip. He knew what Ash said about people not wanting girls to play baseball was true—Drew's older brother was proof of that. And so, he realized, was Ash. Ash wasn't as rude, but he'd made his opinion of having Rachel on the team clear, at least to Carter, and Carter doubted very much that he'd be able to change that opinion.

So why even bother trying? he thought. *It'd be like banging my head against a brick wall.*

Besides, Rachel was strong. Ash had dished out garbage to her now and then, but she'd simply put it aside, dusted off her hands, and walked away.

She doesn't want a battle, he thought. *So I won't be doing her any favors if I pick one with Ash on her account, will I?*

"Listen, Ash," he said finally, "let's just give the whole Rachel thing a rest, okay? We'll take care of it *if* and *when* we need to. Come on. The game is going to start soon."

He turned the corner into the dugout—and almost walked right into Rachel. "Whoops, sorry!" he said. "Didn't see you there."

She gave him a long level look. "No," she said. "I guess you didn't."

CHAPTER
SEVENTEEN

Hey, Liam!"

Melanie poked her head into the dugout and waved her video camera in his face. "I just wanted you to know that I'm moving to another spot. I tried over behind those guys"—she pointed toward the Rattlers dugout—"but the sun was angling right at me so—"

"Just sit behind us, okay?" Liam growled.

"Grouch." She disappeared in a huff.

Liam grimaced. When he had mentioned his idea of videoing his games to Melanie, she'd jumped right on board.

"I need to practice for my film and video class at school," she told him. "This could be perfect!"

It had taken time to get all the permission forms signed by his teammates' parents and Little League officials, so this was her first game. Now she was being such a pain that Liam already regretted having her there.

Then again, if she caught him homering off DiMaggio...well, maybe he wouldn't mind so much after all.

Fifteen minutes later, the game against the Rattlers began. The Pythons were in the field first.

"Bring your best stuff," he said to Spencer.

"I'll try." The pitcher gave Liam a tentative smile. "No, wait, I mean, I'll *do*. Like a Jedi, right?"

Liam frowned. "Save the jokes for later, after we win."

Spencer's smile vanished. He turned and hurried to the mound. He pitched well, but the Rattlers still connected. Luckily, the Pythons retired the side one-two-three thanks to crisp fielding and on-target throws to first.

Phillip returned the favor by striking out the Pythons batters in order.

"Man, I wish I was that good," Liam heard Spencer murmur.

"Me too." The words slipped out of Liam's mouth before he could stop them. He shot Spencer a look of apology. "I just mean because DiMaggio's their best hitter and he's up first. Which reminds me"—he pointed at Jay, Robert, and Rodney—"back up and be ready for the long hit."

"Oh, yes, sir," Robert said. He snapped Liam a mock-salute and then ran onto the field.

Liam snorted. "Nice attitude, huh?" he said to Jay and Rodney.

The outfielders exchanged a look. "Yeah," Rodney said. "I was thinking the same thing." Then they took off after Robert.

Liam moved to the plate and got into his crouch. DiMaggio approached, tapped dirt from his cleats, and surveyed the field. Just before he stepped into the box, the corner of his mouth lifted in a half smile.

Liam's heart skipped a beat. Phillip had seen something he liked out there, he was sure of it. But what?

Is someone out of position? he thought, his eyes darting from Python to Python. Then he saw it. Robert, playing center field, was standing too far toward Jay in right. Phillip was a right-handed batter. If he got a pitch he liked, he could pull the ball left where it could drop into the gap between Rodney and Robert!

It was too late to warn Robert because Spencer was

going into his windup. He threw and—*boom*! Phillip hit the ball with the sweet spot of the bat. And just as Liam had feared, the ball rocketed toward the gap.

"No, no, no!" he cried. Then he gasped. Rodney was sprinting across the grass. No, not sprinting—flying! He covered the distance faster than Liam would have thought possible and then laid his body out, glove reaching, reaching...and capturing the ball at the tip of the leather!

The fans went wild. Every Python was cheering and applauding—except Rodney. He simply stood up, threw the ball back to Spencer, and returned to his position as if making such circus catches were routine.

But Liam knew it was much more than that. That kind of effort and heads-up play was what All-Stars did. With that catch plus his strong performance at the plate, he was sure that come June 15 Rodney would find his name on that roster. He was glad. If anyone on the Pythons deserved to be chosen, it was Rodney.

And yet paired with happiness for his friend was anxiety for himself. The All-Star team fielded fourteen players. Phillip DiMaggio would no doubt get one of the positions. If Rodney claimed one of those slots, that left just twelve. Who would get those?

I will, Liam thought with determination. *After I homer today, one of them will go to me.*

Phillip's out was quickly followed by two more, and the teams switched sides. In the dugout, everyone crowded around Rodney, congratulating him on his catch.

Rodney's father beamed at him and then pushed a batting helmet onto his head. "Go get 'em," he said, the pride in his voice obvious.

"Rod-ney! Rod-ney! Rod-ney!" Sean started chanting. The other Pythons picked up the rhythm, clapping and stomping their feet. Liam cheered along, too. Their encouragement must have helped, because Rodney doubled for the team's first hit.

Not our last, though, Liam thought as he selected a bat. *Look out, DiMaggio, 'cause here I come.*

He stepped into the box and stared at Phillip. Phillip narrowed his eyes. Then he did just what Liam knew he'd do: He touched his chest and then his nose, and then he pointed at Liam.

Liam almost laughed out loud. *Nice try, DiMaggio. But I'm through letting you intimidate me. Now throw me that ball—and get ready to watch it disappear!*

CHAPTER
EIGHTEEN

By the fourth inning of the Hawks-Falcons game, the cool breeze of the morning had died and the temperature had risen fifteen degrees. Carter stood on the mound, looking to put an end to the Falcons' scoring threat.

Suddenly, a rivulet of sweat edged down his brow and into his eye. He wiped it away with the back of his hand. Moments later, his eye began to sting. He rubbed it, but that just made it worse. And when his other eye also began to sting—

"Time!"

Coach Harrison hurried onto the mound. "What's wrong, Carter?"

Carter dug the heels of his hands into his eye sockets.

"Oh, man, they're burning so bad I can't see!" His eyes were streaming tears now, trying to rid themselves of the irritant.

"You got sunscreen in them," the coach guessed. He waved to Seth. "Help him to the restroom. Carter, rinse your eyes until they feel better."

In the men's room, Carter splashed handful after handful of cool water onto his face. Finally, the stinging subsided. He looked up in the mirror and grimaced. The mixture of lotion, sweat, and rubbing had left his eyes flaming red.

"Yikes!" Seth said. "You look like something out of a horror movie."

Carter blinked a few times, hoping it would help. The stinging was gone completely, but the redness remained. When he stepped outside, the bright sunlight made him close his eyes to slits.

He knew before the coach told him that he was done on the mound for the day. He wasn't surprised to hear Rachel warming up. Drew had thrown two days before. Per Little League's pitch-count rules, he was required to rest his arm one more day before taking the mound again. Any number of Hawks could have taken Carter's place, but Rachel was the best candidate because she'd had more practice.

She had more power than some of them, too. And she was using it now. *Whap!* Carter winced as the ball socked into Ash's mitt.

"Yeow, bet that left a mark on his palm," Arthur muttered. "Is it just me, or is she throwing even harder than usual?"

Carter thought Arthur was right. "If she can keep throwing like that and find the target, she'll clean up these last innings and hand us the win on a silver platter," he predicted.

Something of a goofball when not playing, Rachel was no-nonsense when she was on the mound. That was bad news—for the Falcons. She struck out the first batter in six pitches. The second batter connected but knocked the ball straight down in front of home plate. It was a classic Baltimore chop, which Ash picked off on the bounce. One pinpoint throw to first later, the Falcon was sent back to his bench.

"One more, Rachel, one more!" Carter cried.

She didn't get the next Falcon out, or the next. Carter tensed, wondering if Ash would go out to the mound. But the catcher didn't need to, for Rachel retired the side on the next batter.

"Great job, Rach!" Carter praised when she jogged into the dugout. He held up his hand for a high five.

But she just nodded and moved past him to get a drink.

Got her game face on, he thought. Still, he was a little surprised when she didn't sit next to him as she usually did. The Hawks failed to earn a run that inning, their last turn at bat.

"Here you go, Hawks!" Coach Harrison cried as the team moved back onto the field. "Play smart, get the outs, and we'll have a third win in our pockets!"

That win looked a little less certain, though, when Rachel threw the first pitch.

Crack! The Falcon crushed the ball, sending it rocketing just beyond outfielder Remy Werner's reach. Remy scrambled, got his hand on the ball, and heaved it to the cutoff man as quickly as he could. His heads-up play held the runner at third, but with no outs there was a very real possibility that that runner would reach home.

"Come on, Hawks," Carter yelled. "Hold 'em!" The rest of the Hawks picked up the cry.

The second batter singled. Runners on first and third, no outs. The next Falcon laid down a bunt. But Ash and the infielders were anticipating the play. Ash pounced on the ball and hurled it to first for the out. The Falcon at third hadn't budged, so Jerry Tuckerman tried to get the runner out at second. But his throw was too late.

Runners on second and third, one out. One out turned into two with a caught fly ball. Both benches were going wild, chanting for their teams. When Carter saw who the next batter was, however, his cheer stuck in his throat.

A tall boy with an athletic build, Charlie Murray had been an All-Star last year. He had a good swing, but it was his fast feet that earned him the respect of his teammates. More than once in the postseason, he had outrun throws to first. Even if his hit was weak, he could be a threat.

Of course, Coach Harrison knew Charlie, too. Rather than risk Charlie's outrunning a throw, he opted to have Rachel walk him.

Bases loaded, two outs, play to any base.

Now a slim boy with wraparound glasses came to the plate. He missed the first pitch and nicked the second for strike two.

"Come on, Rachel! Sneak one more by him!" Carter bellowed.

She flicked her eyes toward the bench before catching the toss from Ash. Then she stood for what seemed like an eternity. When she finally did throw—

"What the heck was that pitch?" Drew cried in astonishment.

"Whatever it was, it worked!" Remy cheered. "Strike three, baby!"

"Carter, did you see that?" Josh Samuels added, equally amazed.

But Carter was too dumbfounded to answer.

Rachel had just thrown a perfect knuckleball.

CHAPTER

Liam wanted to smash the ball so far that the outfield didn't stand a chance of getting a glove on it. He hit a single instead. There were no outs when Sean came up to bat. Then there were two—Sean hit a grounder that led to a double play from second to first. No doubt the Rattlers would have loved it to be a triple play, but Rodney was far too swift to be thrown out at third.

"Sorry, guys," Sean apologized in the dugout.

"Hey, it happens to all of us," Spencer said.

"Some more than others," Robert muttered from behind Liam.

Liam nodded his head. He'd been thinking the same thing, but he sure wouldn't have said it out loud.

"What was that?"

Liam looked up, surprised to see Spencer and Sean staring at him.

"I didn't say anything," he replied.

The two boys exchanged a glance. Sean shrugged. "Oh, I thought—never mind."

Clint, up after Sean, laced a line drive that was good enough to land him on first—and get Rodney home for the first run of the game. Unfortunately, Jay popped out to end the inning.

The score remained Pythons 1, Rattlers 0 through the bottom of the third. In the top of the fourth, however, the Rattlers crossed home plate twice to make it Rattlers 2, Pythons 1. Liam hoped to even it up with a home run, but instead knocked three long fouls in a row just outside the left-field line. He straightened out the fourth, but by then the third baseman was waiting. He stuck out his glove and made the catch easily.

"Nice try, son," Dr. Driscoll said.

Liam gave him a curt nod. Then, frustrated, he stalked back to the dugout and stood, arms crossed tightly over his chest, against the back wall. A few Pythons glanced his way, but no one spoke to him.

One at bat left, he thought bitterly. *Or, if I'm lucky, two. But what are the chances of that? Zero to none,* he added, shaking his head when Sean made the last out to end the fourth inning.

Neither team scored in the fifth. The Rattlers threatened again in the sixth, putting runners on first and second with just one out. But Alex snared a hopping grounder bare-handed right near third base. He stepped on the bag for out number two and then fired the ball to second. That runner was safe, but the next Rattler grounded out to end the danger.

Rattlers 2, Pythons 1—but now the Pythons were at bat.

"Robert! Rodney! Liam!" Coach Driscoll called, reminding the team of the batting order for their last raps.

Okay, Liam thought, *it's now or never.* He played the scene in his mind over and over. Each time, it ended the same way: a home run that had everyone stamping and cheering his name—and DiMaggio walking off the mound in defeat.

Robert got on base on a fielder's error. Rodney tried to bunt him to second but hit the ball wrong. Instead of dribbling down the baseline, it popped up—and landed smack in Phillip's glove. Phillip whirled around and threw to first in time to get Robert out, too.

Then it was Liam's turn. His heart pounded as he

fitted the helmet onto his head and chose his bat. He dried his sweaty palms on his pants, rolled his shoulders to loosen them up, and then stepped into the box.

He and Phillip locked eyes for a split second before the pitcher began his windup.

Bring it, Liam thought.

The pitch came. He started for it but at the last moment checked his swing. *Thud!*

Had he stopped in time or broken the plane?

"Ball!"

"Good eye, Liam! Good eye!" Coach Driscoll called.

The next pitch fooled him. He swung and missed for a count of one and one. He reached for the next pitch and missed that, too. But the fourth—

Pow!

It was a home run. Liam was sure of it. He took off down the base path at an easy trot, grinning widely. Then he heard the first-base coach.

"Are you crazy? *Move!*" Devon screamed.

Liam whipped his head around. His jaw dropped. The ball had hit the ground—inside the fence!

"Go! Go! Go!" Devon hollered. "Before they pick it up!"

Liam was already sprinting. He rounded first. Reached second. Saw Brian Benson, the third-base coach, frantically wheeling his arm. He put the pedal to the metal and hit third.

"They missed the cutoff man! *Run!*" Brian bellowed.

Liam ran, faster and harder than he ever had in his life. The Rattlers catcher was waiting at the plate, mitt up. Then suddenly, the catcher jumped. The throw to home was wild!

Liam tore up the last few yards of dirt. Phillip, backing up the catcher, scrambled to find the ball in the dust. Five feet before the plate, Liam dropped into a slide. Phillip tossed the ball to the catcher. The catcher nabbed it, swung his glove around and down and missed!

"Safe!" the umpire yelled, fanning his arms out to either side.

"Yes!" Liam leaped to his feet and pumped the air with his fist.

"Hold it!" someone cried. The field umpire was racing in, waving his arms through the air.

Liam froze, arm still in midair.

"I'm sorry, son," the umpire said, his voice full of sympathy.

Coach Driscoll hurried onto the field to see what was happening. The field umpire explained, saying that the Cobras' coach had appealed the missed base, insisting that Liam's foot had landed near the bag, but not on it at any time. Liam's stomach dropped. He felt helpless as he watched what happened next—the ball went back to the mound, where it was called back into play and then thrown to the second baseman. He stepped on the base, and the umpire made the ruling. Instead of making a run, Liam had made the final out.

He stood rooted to the spot. Then the storm brewing inside him all game long finally erupted. He spun on his heel, walked stiff-legged with humiliation to the dugout, and yanked off his helmet.

The moment it happened, he wished it back. Even before he saw the look on Coach Driscoll's face, he knew he'd crossed a line. The question was, would he be able to cross back? Was his unacceptable behavior the end of his time as a Python?

CHAPTER
TWENTY

I knew she was trouble," Ash said, "but I still can't believe she stole your pitch."

It was the day after the Hawks' win over the Falcons, and Ash and Carter were having a game of catch in the Joneses' backyard.

"Me neither." Carter took the ball out of his glove and threw it back in. Again and again, harder and harder. Finally, he hurled the ball to Ash.

"What makes it even worse," Ash said, "is that Mr. Delaney taught it to her."

Carter was silent. That was the part he didn't understand. Not once during their sessions had the pitching coach mentioned that he was working with Rachel, too. But he knew it was true because that's what he'd heard Rachel tell Coach Harrison.

In the dugout after the win, the coach had taken her aside and asked her about the pitch. Carter was close enough to hear her replies, as was Ash.

"I heard about the knuckleball from Carter," she explained. "The next time I saw Matt Delaney, I asked him about it."

"I thought Mr. Delaney's name was Mark," Ash whispered to Carter.

Carter shushed him. He wanted to hear what else Rachel had to say.

"He offered to show me how to throw the knuckleball," Rachel continued. She shrugged. "I guess I'm a fast learner."

"I see," Mr. Harrison said. "For the record, I would have appreciated a heads-up that you were learning something new. It's important that you receive the right instruction at this stage."

He glanced sideways at Carter and Ash, who pretended to examine something on Ash's chest protector. "It's also important that you keep your teammates in the loop. Ash had no way of knowing you were going to throw a knuckleball. Throwing a pitch your catcher isn't expecting can be dangerous. Not only that, I'm sure the Hawks bull pen would welcome the chance to work on that pitch and others with you—under proper coaching supervision, of course."

Now Rachel looked Carter's way. "Really? I'm not so sure."

"Why do you say that?" Mr. Harrison asked sharply.

Carter kept his eyes glued to the chest protector, not daring to look at either Rachel or Ash. *Would she bring up the snide remarks she'd overheard Ash make about her? What would Ash do if she did? What would the coach do?*

But after a moment, she smiled. "Are you kidding? It's crowded enough in there already, with Drew and Carter and Ash and Leonard," she said. Then she shifted her gaze past Mr. Harrison and brightened. "Look! There's my pitching coach now. I forgot he was going to be here today. I guess if you have any more questions about what he's been teaching me, you could ask him. Better hurry, though. Looks like he's about to leave."

Carter spotted Mr. Delaney helping someone into his car. He waved. The coach waved back, but to Carter's disappointment, he didn't come over. Instead, he got into his car and drove off.

"Think Rachel will be there when we meet with Mr. Delaney tomorrow?" Ash asked now.

Carter held up his glove, and Ash threw him the ball. "Guess we'll find out," he said.

But they didn't, because that night, the coach canceled their session. "I have to take my son to a doctor's appointment," he explained to Carter. "I'll be in touch to reschedule."

The coach wasn't the only cancellation Carter had that night. Liam texted before dinner to say he wouldn't be able to video-chat. Carter texted back to find out why, but Liam never answered.

"It was weird," he said to his father when he came downstairs later. "First he blows me off for the call and then he ignores my text."

Mr. Jones was at the computer. "I think I might know what's going on. Come see." He tapped a few keys. A video appeared. "Aunt Amanda sent this earlier. It's footage of Liam's last game. Melanie took it." He clicked PLAY.

The video started with Liam hitting a blazing, high fly ball.

"He homered—oh, wait, no, he didn't," Carter said when Liam suddenly began running instead of trotting.

Carter saw Liam race to second, third, and then elude the catcher's tag at home. He saw the field umpire hurry in and heard him report the appeal. And then he saw what had his father so concerned.

"He acted that way?!" Carter said, aghast. "Did he—did he get thrown out of the game?"

Mr. Jones paused the video. "No, but Amanda says there might be disciplinary action." He shook his head in consternation. "Why would Liam be that way?"

"Hold on. Look." Carter pointed to a tiny figure frozen on the screen. "That's Phillip DiMaggio. If Liam thought he'd homered off him, he would have been beyond psyched. So when the run was taken away because of the missed base..."

"Ah." His father nodded knowingly. "That home run meant a lot to him, I guess."

"That one, and all the others he's been trying to make this season."

Mr. Jones cocked his head to one side. "Sounds like there's more to this story."

Carter told his father about Liam's quest to be the home run king. "He thinks it's the only way to prove himself in his new league," he finished.

"Mmmm." Mr. Jones sat back in his chair and laced his fingers over his stomach. "Well, now I have a better idea of what Liam's been struggling with. Which brings me to my next question: What went wrong at your game yesterday?"

Carter picked at his pant leg. "You noticed, huh?"

121

"Hard not to, the way you were stomping around here."

"Okay, so you know I've been working on that pitch?"

"The knuckleball, yes."

"Well," Carter said, "my teammate Rachel threw it yesterday. Not me. Her. She went behind my back to learn it."

"And you feel betrayed by that," his father guessed.

"Yeah, wouldn't you?" Carter asked indignantly.

"What does Rachel say about it?"

Carter lifted a shoulder and let it drop.

His father studied him thoughtfully. "You know, there are two sides to most stories." He gestured toward the video. "If we didn't know anything about Liam or his history with Phillip, we would think he was just some kid throwing a tantrum. Maybe you need to listen to Rachel's side before you decide she's the enemy."

CHAPTER
TWENTY-ONE

I don't feel good," Liam rasped. "I think I need to stay home from school."

"Nonsense."

Liam's mother opened his drapes with a furious yank. "It's no good trying to hide from what happened," she said, not unkindly. "You have to face it head-on, starting today. Now, up and at 'em. The McGrath bus service leaves in twenty minutes."

Liam heaved a sigh. He hated to admit it, but he knew his mother was right. The longer he put off dealing with what he'd done, the worse it would be.

And it was already bad; he knew that. Yanking his helmet had been stupid, and he cringed whenever he thought of that moment. He cringed more when he remembered the shocked looks on his teammates' faces and the hard tone in Dr. Driscoll's voice.

"Liam," his coach had said. "Take a seat. Pythons, give us a moment."

Dr. Driscoll hadn't chewed him out. He'd simply told Liam that the league's Board of Directors would undoubtedly discuss whether to discipline him. "It's your first offense, so perhaps they'll keep that in mind," he added. "I certainly hope it's your last."

"Yes, sir." Liam had wanted to say more but couldn't get the words out. He'd remained silent throughout the postgame wrap. His mother and sister had whispered in the front seat on the ride home, but he kept quiet— then, and throughout much of Sunday.

But now it was Monday morning. He couldn't hide anymore. So he got up and dressed. Ten minutes later, he was downstairs in the kitchen, eating breakfast.

Melanie came in a moment later. "Oh. Hi." She stood awkwardly and then said, "I'm sorry about—you know. I really am."

Liam hunched over his cereal. "Yeah. Me too."

"Mom making you face it head-on?"

He nodded grimly.

She slid onto the stool next to him and peeled a

banana. "Want some advice? Rip the bandage off quickly, all at once, not little by little."

He pushed his bowl away, no longer hungry. "Another fortune-cookie saying?"

"Speaking of which," she added, "did you remember the first one? About watching where you step when you climb the ladder?"

Liam was about to ask her to stop speaking in riddles, but their mother breezed into the kitchen. "All fed? Good," she said. "Dishes in the dishwasher, peels in the trash, kids in the car, and we're off."

The ride to school seemed shorter than usual to Liam that morning. After his mother dropped him off, he climbed the concrete stairs and pushed open the double doors into the building with mounting dread. Inside, he walked slowly toward the cafeteria. That was where all the students gathered before the first bell sent them to their homerooms. And that was where he knew he'd see Rodney, Sean, and Spencer sitting together at their usual table.

Sure enough, they were there, speaking in low voices. When they saw Liam, they stopped talking. He swallowed hard but didn't slow his step.

Time to rip the bandage off, he thought.

"Hey." It came out as a squeak. He cleared his throat and tried again. "Hey. Hi."

All three regarded him for a long moment. Then Rodney said, "Doing okay, man?"

Liam sat down and stared at the Formica tabletop. "Not really. I screwed up royally, didn't I?"

"Yep," Rodney said. Sean and Spencer stayed quiet.

Liam lifted his head and looked at them—and suddenly he understood what Melanie meant about watching where he stepped.

"I messed up before, though," he said. "I've been a pretty lousy teammate lately, haven't I?"

Spencer drew a shape on the tabletop with his fingertip but didn't answer. Sean did.

"You've been acting a lot like Robert."

Liam flinched at the comparison. Then he put his head in his hands. "Oh, man. How can you guys stand to be around me?" He'd meant the question sincerely. But to his surprise and relief, they laughed.

"It hasn't been easy," Spencer admitted.

"What was going on with you, anyway?" Sean wanted to know.

So Liam took a deep breath and tried to explain— about wanting to make the All-Star team, about thinking he needed to do something spectacular to stand out, about wanting to put his strikeout behind him once and for all. "Hitting homers seemed like the perfect solution to all that," he finished.

"Yeah, I can see your logic," Sean said. "It's warped, but I can still see it."

"I have a question," Spencer cut in. "What strikeout are you talking about?"

Liam stared at him in astonishment. "Last year's World Series? Pitch thrown by the same guy who makes you nervous—Phillip DiMaggio?"

Spencer screwed up his face. "Phillip DiMaggio doesn't make me nervous."

"But you said—whenever he showed up at a game, you got all nutty," Liam protested.

"I get nutty when my *grandfather* shows up," Spencer corrected.

Liam suddenly remembered the stern-faced old man with the almond-shaped eyes he'd seen sitting behind Phillip during the game against the Cobras. He asked Spencer if that man was his grandfather.

Spencer nodded. "He pitched in the Minors, and I'm not talking Little League Minors."

"Whoa," Liam and the Driscolls said.

"Yeah. He taught me a lot, but talk about pressure." Spencer shot Liam a sheepish look. "And then when your sister showed up with the video camera, that didn't do much for me, either."

"You didn't want to be filmed?"

Spencer blushed. "It wasn't that. It's—dude, your sister is kind of pretty."

"Gross!" Liam said.

"So now you know *my* deal," Spencer said hurriedly. "What is this strikeout you're talking about?"

"Oh, it wasn't just a strikeout," Rodney drawled. "It was a colossal miss."

"Huge," Sean agreed, "and it was followed by the best pirouette down into the dirt ever seen in the history of baseball."

"The kind of embarrassing moment you never recover from," Rodney added. "Unless of course...you do." He grinned at Liam. "Have you?"

"You know what?" Liam said slowly. "I think I just did."

Spencer crossed his arms and scowled. "Fine," he said in a huff. "Don't tell me about it."

After school, Liam went home with the Driscolls so he could apologize to their father in person.

"I appreciate this, Liam," Dr. Driscoll said when Liam finished. "And I expect you to apologize to the rest of the Pythons, of course."

Liam nodded. He'd already planned to do just that.

The coach scrubbed his face with his hands. "I was aware of your past difficulties with Phillip. But I wasn't aware that you were still having issues with him. I wish you'd talked to me. I might have been able to help before things got out of hand. By the way, the league has decided not to take any action against you, which is quite generous, if you ask me."

Dr. Driscoll blew out his breath then and shook his head. "Before Saturday, I would have said you were on track to make the All-Star team. But now, I'm afraid you're facing an uphill battle. If you want to be selected, you'll have to give the rest of the season everything you've got. And you'll have to prove to me and your teammates that you're the kind of player we want representing this league."

Liam nodded. He knew he had a lot of work to do.

CHAPTER
TWENTY-TWO

Carter had a restless night after talking with his father. He knew what he should do—talk to Rachel—but somehow, he couldn't make himself pick up the phone.

I'll see how things are at practice, he told himself. *If she acts normal, I will, too.*

The first thing he noticed when he saw her at the field on Tuesday was her expression. It was serious and businesslike. When she spotted Carter, she nodded politely and then turned away. Throughout practice, she spoke only when necessary. And when the practice ended, she left with a few simple good-byes, leaving more than one Hawk puzzled.

Not normal, Carter thought. A worm of guilt crept into his brain. He pushed it away. *I didn't do anything wrong. She did.* But the worm refused to leave.

The Hawks faced the Kestrels on Friday afternoon. Drew was on the mound with Leonard behind the plate. Carter played third base, and Ash was in the outfield. So was Rachel. Carter wondered if she would return to her usual self. She didn't.

The Hawks lost 6–2, their first defeat of the season.

"You did a lot right out there," Coach Harrison commented after the game. Then his forehead creased. "But something was missing. There was no energy, no extra spark." He spread his hands. "I can't coach that into you. It's either there or it's not. Let's hope it returns for our next game."

On Saturday afternoon, Ash and Carter met for a bike ride.

"I don't know what the coach was talking about yesterday," Ash said to Carter. "I thought we were more focused than we've ever been."

"What do you mean?"

"Well, there was less goofing off in the dugout, for one thing. Less chatter in the outfield, too."

Carter snorted. "That's funny, coming from the king of chatter!"

"That's different," Ash defended himself. "My chatter helps."

"Actually, it doesn't," Carter blurted out. "Not when you're behind the plate and I'm pitching, anyway."

Ash looked surprised. "Really? Why didn't you tell me that sooner?"

"I did! Way back before the season started."

"Oh. Well, you should have told me again." Then he looked pointedly at Carter. "And if there's anyone else whose chatter or jokes or clowning around bother you, you should tell him—or *her*—to stop, too."

Carter hit the brakes so hard, he skidded to a stop. "That's what was missing!"

Ash braked, too. "What?"

"Rachel's chatter. Her jokes. Her clowning around in the dugout. I know she drives you nuts, but she makes the rest of us laugh. When we laugh together, we work better as a team. I don't know why, but I know it's true. Want proof? Rachel was all serious yesterday, and we lost." He smiled. "Face it, man. She's the spark."

He wheeled his bike around then and started pedaling.

"Where are you going?" Ash called.

"To Rachel's house! See you!"

When Rachel saw who was at her front door, she looked surprised, and then wary. "What do you want?"

"I want to talk about what happened at the game," Carter told her.

"I know what happened," she said, leaning against the doorjamb. "We lost."

"Not that game. The one where you threw the knuckleball."

Rachel lifted her chin. "What about it?"

"Why didn't you tell me you were learning it? Why'd you throw it?"

Her blue eyes narrowed. "I threw it because I was mad at you."

"What? Why?"

"Because you weren't very nice to me."

Carter's jaw dropped. "I never said anything!"

"No kidding. Ash was talking about me behind my back, and you never said anything." She emphasized the last four words, hammering them home.

Carter bit his lip. "I thought you could handle it."

"Oh, I can, believe me," she said. "But it would have been nice to hear you stick up for me, too."

They were quiet for a long moment. Then Carter said, "I'm sorry."

After another moment, Rachel smiled ruefully. "I'm sorry, too. Throwing the knuckleball was pretty underhanded."

Carter shot her a grin. "Like softball?"

She laughed. "Yeah, like softball." Then she glanced at a nearby clock and said, "Want to meet the guy who taught me the pitch?"

"I already know him, remember?"

She waggled her eyebrows. "You think you do, but you don't. Come on."

Mystified, Carter waited while she got her bike. He followed her to the high school. In the parking lot, Carter saw Mr. Delaney's car. It was pulled into a handicapped spot and had a tag hanging from the rearview mirror.

"Who—?" he started to ask.

"Just come on," Rachel urged. "I'm already a little late."

She led him to the baseball field where a practice was in session. When Carter saw the players, he stopped short. "They're…" He tried but failed to find the word he was looking for.

"Challenged," Rachel supplied. "Carter, meet the Challenger team."

Spread out across the field he could see children and teens of various ages, and with various physical and mental disabilities. Two were in wheelchairs. One was blind. Others had Down syndrome or other forms of developmental delays. He recognized one girl from school. She waved and he waved back.

"Ms. Warburton, it's about time!"

A man in a wheelchair rolled toward them, smiling. Carter had never seen him before, and yet he looked strangely familiar.

"Carter Jones," Rachel said. "I'd like you to meet the guy who taught me the knuckleball."

"So you're Carter," the man said, extending his hand for Carter to shake. "My dad's told me a lot about you. I'm Matt Delaney."

Carter's eyes widened in disbelief. "Matt Delaney? You're Mr. Delaney's son? The pitcher who helped the high school team win three championships?"

Matt laughed. "Well, that was a few years ago now. Before..." He tapped the arm of his wheelchair. "Anyway, now I work with this group, with my dad's help." He nodded toward the dugout. Carter glanced over and saw Mr. Delaney sitting with a few players. "And I've got great peer volunteers, too, like Rachel." He cocked his head to one side. "You going to join, too? We can always use another baseball pal."

Rachel answered for him. "Not this year, Matt. Unless I'm wrong, Carter's going to have a really long baseball season this year." She gave him her best smile. "In fact, I predict right now that he and his future All-Star teammates will make it to the World Series again!"

Matt laughed. "And what about you? Will you be going, too?"

Rachel shrugged. "Only time will tell. Now come on, Carter. There are more people I want you to meet!"

CHAPTER
TWENTY-THREE

After his talk with Coach Driscoll, Liam thought long and hard about how to erase the bad impression he'd made on his teammates. He decided there was just one solution: work hard on his game and on his attitude.

So he gave extra effort during practices. He cheered when a teammate went up to bat. He applauded good plays and commiserated when something went wrong. He shared handshakes and laughs and disappointments. And with each passing day, he put his poor behavior further behind him—but he never forgot what he'd done. It was too important a lesson to leave behind.

The Pythons enjoyed a winning season, ending tied

for the top spot with the Rattlers. A week before school got out in June, the two teams met for a playoff to determine the league champion. Liam's heart hammered in his chest when he faced Phillip DiMaggio at the plate. But it was a good feeling, an adrenaline rush filled with determination not desperation. He blasted a stand-up double off the Rattlers pitcher and then was batted home to score the tying run. One run later, the Pythons were crowned league champs.

Liam didn't end up as the home run king—Rodney surprised him by claiming that title—but he didn't mind. He had played his best in the second half of the season, and nobody could do more than that. Even better, he'd made friendships he felt sure would last for a long time.

And yet...each night before he climbed into bed, he looked at a photograph that hung above his desk. It was a bird's-eye view of his hometown in Pennsylvania. The photo showed buildings and streets, forests and fields. He always zeroed in on two tiny houses that sat on the same road. He used to live in one house; Carter still lived in the other.

From there, his gaze moved to a spot behind their houses. Hidden from view beneath some trees was the hideout he and Carter had discovered years ago. He wondered if his cousin ever visited that spot and when he might see it and Carter again.

Two days before the All-Star team roster was announced, Liam sat waiting for Carter to sign on to video-chat. He was just about to give up when the alarm began.

"Finally," he said when his cousin's image appeared. "Where've you been?"

"Hey, I'm here now, aren't I?" Carter answered.

Liam tilted his head sideways, puzzled by something he saw on the screen behind Carter. "Yeah, but where's 'here'? You're not in your room. It looks familiar, but— where *are* you?"

Carter smothered a laugh. As Liam was about to ask what was so funny, he heard the doorbell chime.

"Liam, can you get that?" his father called.

"Can't you? I'm talking to Carter!"

"I really need you to see who's at the door!"

Liam groaned. "Carter, can you hang on? There's someone at the front door."

At that, Carter grinned. "Yeah, I know. Want to see who it is?"

Before Liam could reply, the image on his laptop screen whirled around in a blur. When it came to a stop, Liam found himself looking at—

"That's the door to my house. How——?"

Suddenly, Liam understood why the background behind Carter had looked so familiar. He bolted out of his chair, raced down the stairs, and practically tore the front door off its hinges.

"Dork!" he yelled.

"Doofus!" Carter yelled back.

Carter shoved his laptop into his mother's arms seconds before Liam crushed him in a bear hug. "I can't believe you're here!" Liam cried.

"I can't believe you're squeezing the air out of my lungs," Carter gasped.

"And I can't believe you're both standing in my way," Carter's mother said. She pushed by them into the hallway, put the laptop on a table, and shouted, "Amanda! Amanda, where are you?"

Someone in the cellar screamed. Footsteps pounded up the stairs. The door to the basement flung open and Liam's mother rushed into the hall. Her jaw dropped when she saw her sister, and then the two women were hugging and screaming together.

"I can't believe it!" Liam's mother shouted over and over.

Liam and Carter exchanged glances.

"Women," Liam said, shaking his head.

"No kidding," Carter agreed.

They disappeared upstairs to Liam's room. "Okay, so I can't believe it, either," Liam confessed, sitting on one of the two twin beds. "How long are you staying?"

"We're heading back in five days. That's when, you know, All-Star practices start. Not that I know whether I made the team or anything," he added hurriedly. "But my folks thought it'd be smarter to play it safe, just in case."

Liam nodded. "You know you're going to make the team, right? It was thanks to you and that knuckleball that the Hawks were the league champs for the second year in a row."

"Not just me," Carter protested. "Everyone did their part, you know that." Then he grinned. "But I have to admit, I like ending the season on top again. Don't you?"

"Definitely." Then Liam thought of something. "Hold on, how are you going to find out about All-Stars? You'll be here!"

"Coach Harrison said he'd call here one way or the other. What about you?"

Liam gave a half smile. "Oh, I don't think *I'll* be getting a call from Coach Harrison this year," he said. Then his smile vanished. "Maybe not from Coach Driscoll, either. Of course, that would be my own fault. I forgot to watch my step when I was climbing the ladder."

"What are you, a fortune-cookie saying?"

"Nah, that's something Melanie said once. I should have listened to her. Don't ever tell her I said that." He flopped backward onto his bed and then lifted his head to peer at Carter. "Why didn't you talk some sense into me?"

Carter snorted. "Like I've ever been able to do that?"

"Hmmm, good point. Let's change the subject."

They talked about everything and nothing until their mothers called up to let them know pizza had arrived. Only later, when they were in bed with the lights out, did the subject of the All-Star announcements come up again.

"You know, it'll actually be okay if I don't make the team," Liam said into the darkness.

"Yeah? Why's that?"

Liam rolled onto his side toward Carter's bed. "Think about it. Me? On a team with Phillip DiMaggio? Yikes!"

There was just enough light in the room for Liam to see the appalled look on his cousin's face. "I never even thought of that! But you're sure he's going to make the team?"

"Oh, yeah, he'll make it. It kills me to say so, but he's really good."

Carter was quiet for a minute and then said, "Better than me?"

"You know you're first in my book," Liam replied loyally. "But there's another reason why it'd be okay if I don't make the team. I won't ever have to play against you."

Carter laughed. "Like that would ever happen!"

"It could if I made the team!" Liam insisted.

"Not a chance. When's the last time the same two teams reached the U.S. Championship? Or even the World Series tournament? I'll tell you when—never!"

"Doesn't mean it can't happen," Liam said stubbornly.

Both boys were silent for a while, each lost in his own thoughts. Liam wondered if Carter had fallen asleep, but then his cousin said, "It couldn't happen, could it?"

Liam rolled away. "Nothing's impossible."

CHAPTER
TWENTY-FOUR

Carter was woken up by the smell of bacon in his nostrils—and the feel of bacon rubbing against his nose.

"Wake up, dork," Liam said in a singsong voice. "Or the bacon fairy will touch you with her magic wand again!"

Carter shoved Liam's hand away and sat up. "And to think I missed you."

"Come on," Liam said. "The moms say we can sleep out tonight. Let's go get the tent set up."

"Can't I eat first?"

"Sure." Liam tossed the slice of bacon at him. "Enjoy!"

Half an hour and one real breakfast later, the boys

were in the backyard puzzling over the tent directions. When they had just figured out that pole A fit through slot 4, someone called Liam's name. Carter looked up to see three boys walking into the yard.

"No way!" the youngest of the three gasped. "It's Carter Jones!"

Carter blinked. "Um, hi?"

The boy stuck out his hand. "I'm Spencer Park. I watched you pitch in the U.S. Championship last year. You were great! No, better than great, awesome! In fact, I thought for sure Mid-Atlantic was going to win the whole thing. And I bet you would have, too, if your teammate hadn't struck out. Don't get me wrong, I was glad that West won, but man, I felt bad for that kid." He shook his head ruefully.

Carter stared at Spencer and then looked at Liam. His cousin was trying his best not to laugh. Liam and the Driscolls still hadn't clued Spencer in about Liam's big strikeout. And he obviously hadn't matched Liam's face to the video!

"Yeah," Carter said slowly, "a lot of people felt bad for him. But don't worry. He's doing okay now."

"You still play ball with him, huh?"

Carter bit his lip to keep from cracking up. "Not as

often as I'd like." Then he turned to the other boys, both of whom were attempting to control their mirth, too.

"Hi, I'm Rodney Driscoll," the tall, dark-haired boy said. "That's my brother, Sean. Believe it or not, we're—"

"Don't tell me," Carter interrupted, grinning. "Twins?"

Now the brothers did laugh. "Guess Liam told you about our favorite gag, huh?"

Carter glanced at his cousin. "Yeah, and a lot more about you guys, too. Congrats on the home run title, Rodney."

"Thanks. Need some help with that?"

Liam handed him the directions. "All we can get!"

While the boys worked on the tent, Liam told them how Carter had surprised him yesterday.

"Too bad you can't stay longer," Spencer said. "But it's more important for you to start practicing with your All-Star team." He shot Liam a smile. "After all, it can take a while for new teammates to find their groove."

Liam laughed and then cupped his hands around his mouth. "Groove? Anybody see a groove around here? Hello, I'm looking for a groove!" Rodney, Sean, and Spencer immediately joined in.

While they were laughing, Carter busied himself with the tent poles. He felt odd not being in on the joke with Liam. But he shrugged it off. Liam didn't know the jokes he shared with Rachel or Ash, either.

Once the tent was finally up, Sean suggested they go to the ballpark for a game of pitch, hit, and run. "Wiffle balls, all right? Because this is just for fun," he added. "Some of us are done for the season, remember."

Carter looked at him in surprise. "You don't know that. The All-Star announcements don't come out until tomorrow. You could start playing again next week."

Sean laughed. "Thanks for the vote of confidence, man, but I'm not holding out any hope. I mean, I'm a great guy and all, but no chance I'm on the roster." He turned and punched Rodney in the arm. "Unlike some guys I know, huh, bro?"

Carter saw Liam stiffen. "Hey, why don't you guys ride ahead to the field?" he said. "Liam, you go get the gear. I'll go ask your dad if I can borrow his bike."

The Driscolls and Spencer agreed and left. Inside the house, Carter turned to Liam and said, "Okay, first off, I can't believe Spencer has no clue who you are."

"You and me both. Not that I have a problem with him not knowing!"

"And secondly, Sean can't know for sure that Rodney's on the team."

Liam looked down. "I know, I know. But still, if he

thought I had a chance, why wouldn't he have said so?" He shook his head. "Maybe that was his way of warning me that I didn't make it. His dad is the All-Star coach, remember. Maybe he overheard him say something or—"

"Okay, that's crazy and you know it," Carter interjected. "Now come on, let's go take your mind off baseball for a while"—he grinned—"by playing some baseball for a while."

Twenty minutes later Liam and Carter reached the field. Sean, Rodney, and Spencer had run into Jay on their way to the park and invited him to join in. Spencer, Sean, and Rodney went into the field first. Liam offered to shag balls batters missed. Jay handed Carter the bat and waved him to the box.

Carter got into his stance. He was suddenly aware of everyone watching him. *I'm the new kid,* he thought. *They don't know what I can do. Well, I'll show them!*

And at that moment, it dawned on him: That's what Liam had felt at the beginning of the season. He wanted to drop the bat and tell his cousin he understood. But then Spencer threw the ball, and there was no time to do anything else but swing.

Whack!

CHAPTER
TWENTY-FIVE

A bright beam of sunlight shone through an opening in the tent and woke Liam the next morning. He looked around. Carter's sleeping bag was empty. He thought about rolling over and going back to sleep, but then he remembered what day it was.

June 15: All-Star Announcement Day.

He shoved his sleeping bag aside and hurried into the house. Melanie was sitting at the kitchen island eating a bowl of sliced strawberries.

"Eesh, look what the cat dragged in," she said when she saw him.

He gave a tremendous yawn and then sat down.

"Where's Carter?" he asked, stealing a berry from her bowl and popping it into his mouth.

"On the phone in Dad's office."

Liam leaped up. "Why didn't you tell me that before?"

"You didn't ask!"

Liam ran down the hall to his father's office.

"Okay, yep, yep, no problem," Carter was saying. "Right. See you in a few days. Bye." He handed his cell phone to his mother, who spoke a little longer and then hung up.

"Well?" Liam exploded. "Did you make it?"

Carter laughed. "That was just Dad. I called him to see how Lucky Boy was doing. He said—"

Just then, another cell phone rang nearby. Mrs. Jones started. "That can't be your father. It must be Coach Harrison! I gave him my number. But where did I put that phone?"

Her cell rang again. Carter jumped up. "Quick! Follow that sound!"

After a frantic search, they found the phone on the table in the living room. "Hello? Yes, he's right here. One moment." Mrs. Jones held out the phone to Carter. "It's the coach."

Carter put the phone to his ear, turned away, and

started pacing. "Hello? Yes, sir, California's been great. Liam's good, too. No, he hasn't heard anything yet."

Suddenly he stopped moving and was quiet. An eternity seemed to pass before he spoke again.

"Thank you, sir. Thank you so much! I'll see you Wednesday, three o'clock sharp."

Then he hung up. "I'm an All-Star!" he cried, his face wreathed in a giant smile.

Liam pumped his fist in the air. "Yes!"

Carter spent the next hour calling and texting his friends back home. Mrs. Jones contacted her husband with the good news and then went on the computer to find out the upcoming tournament dates. Liam got dressed and ate breakfast. He and Carter rolled up the sleeping bags, cleaned out the tent, and then packed it away so they could play catch out back.

"Show me that knuckleball," Liam requested when they were warmed up. When Carter threw it, however, Liam found he could barely follow the ball's movement. He missed the catch the first time—and three more times until he finally got a glove on the fourth.

"Whew!" he exclaimed. "Hope I never have to try to hit one of those!"

After lunch, they played video games and Ping-Pong

in the basement. Liam got out his pin collection, and they looked through them together. All the while, Liam kept one ear out, listening for the phone to ring.

But it didn't.

When no one was looking, he picked up the receiver and checked the dial tone. It was working, so he quickly replaced it in case someone was trying to call.

But no one did.

Dinner that night was a quiet affair.

"I've got an idea," Mr. McGrath said as he passed a bowl of salad. "How about a trip to the amusement park tomorrow? They've got some great roller coasters and other thrill rides designed to make old people like me scream in terror. What do you say?"

"Sounds good to me," Liam's mother agreed brightly. Her sister nodded.

"I'll go if Liam wants to," Carter said.

Liam looked at their expectant faces. He didn't feel like going on a roller coaster. But sitting around the house, he knew, would be even worse.

"Sure," he said. "Let's go."

After dinner, the McGraths and the Joneses settled down in the living room to watch a movie. It was one Liam had seen before. Midway through, he stood up.

"I'm going to head up to—"

He was cut off by a sudden loud knock on the door.

"Who could that be at this hour?" Mrs. McGrath wondered as she hurried to open it.

Rodney and Sean burst into the room, followed by their father.

"Liam! Liam!" the brothers cried. "You're in!"

"I'm—*what*?"

Dr. Driscoll walked over and held out his hand. "Congratulations, Liam. You're an All-Star."

It took a moment for the news to sink in. Then Liam gave a whoop and started dancing around the house. "I don't believe it!"

"Believe it!" Carter yelled. He, Sean, and Rodney started dancing, too.

"But it's eight o'clock at night," Liam's mother protested. "Why didn't you tell him sooner?"

"I didn't know until now," Dr. Driscoll apologized. "You see, Liam wasn't on the roster originally."

Liam stopped dancing. "I wasn't?"

"There are fourteen All-Star slots," the coach continued. "You were fifteenth in votes. Then one of the boys declined his spot. The committee had to make a choice—go with just thirteen players or move you up. It was a very long discussion. But in the end, we agreed to invite you to join the team."

He handed Liam a piece of paper. "Here's the roster. I'll be in touch with practice information. Come on, boys, time to head home."

"Look under *D*," Rodney whispered on his way out the door.

Liam glanced down and saw *Driscoll, Rodney*. Above that listing was another familiar name: *DiMaggio, Phillip*.

CHAPTER
TWENTY-SIX

All right, All-Stars, we have just ten days to get in sync for the District tournament," Coach Harrison said. "So take a look at one another. If you don't know someone, go meet him. If you know everybody, well, introduce them to me because I'm still trying to put names with faces!"

Carter and his new teammates laughed. Then they did as their coach instructed. Carter recognized most of the boys, but he suspected Ash didn't. To his amazement, however, the catcher greeted each one by name.

"You're Freddie Detweiler, right?" he said to a rangy boy with prominent teeth and stick-straight hair. "You played second base for the Falcons."

"Luke Armstrong! Great name for a pitcher." That got a shiny smile from a boy with braces. "I'm Ash. I'll be your catcher sometimes, I guess.

"Hang on, two Charlies and you're both outfielders. Okay, let me see—you're Charlie Santiago and you're Charlie Murray. Maybe we should call you Murray to avoid confusion." Charlie Murray raised his thick eyebrows in alarm. Ash grinned. "Hmm, how about Chuck instead?"

"How do you know these guys?" Carter asked at one point. "I'm not sure who they are and I've lived here all my life!"

"It's my job as catcher to know the opposition," Ash replied. "I've been studying them all season. Remember my binder with the info on all the teams?"

When Ash mentioned it, Carter recalled seeing him with that binder. "Impressive," he commented.

"I marked the guys I thought might show up here." Ash puffed out his chest. "Got most of them right, too."

"Was I on the list?" Carter asked, only half-joking.

"Since last January!" Ash said.

It was only the first practice, but with the tournament looming, Coach Harrison and his assistants, Coach Walker and Coach Filbert, got right down to business. First they warmed the players up with some stretches and then jogged with them around the field.

"Glad to see that no one's huffing and puffing," Coach Harrison said. "Except maybe Coach Walker!" he added with a smile.

Next they told the boys to pair off for a throwing drill. Carter and Ash went together. Carter stood about twelve yards away and in the ready position for an over-the-belt catch—hands chest high, thumbs close together, glove open and waiting. Ash threw to him fifteen times, with Carter resetting in the ready position after he threw the ball back. Then they switched roles and Ash caught.

"Now before we change to a below-the-belt catch," Coach Harrison said, "Carter's line move down one place so you're with a new partner." When the shift was complete, he set the drill in motion. "Remember, now the little fingers are close, glove pocket is toward the ground, and bend your knees, not your backs!"

The catching drills were followed by practice fielding ground balls. The assistant coaches knelt and bounced grounders to the boys while Mr. Harrison called out corrections.

"Pivot with that throw, Ron!"

"Keith, get your caboose down or the ball will roll through your legs instead of into your glove."

"Heads up, eyes on the ball, all of you!"

It was a fast-paced drill that had them moving through the lines quickly and efficiently. After ground balls, they took turns running and catching fly balls thrown high into the air by the coaches. Carter was perspiring freely when Coach Harrison instructed them to put their gloves in the dugout and line up at home plate for a base-running drill.

"Man, this is awesome!" Ash said enthusiastically as he tossed his glove onto the bench.

Carter laughed. "You're in a good mood today."

"Who wouldn't be? It's only day one, we've never played together before, and we're all moving together like clockwork."

Carter nodded in agreement. "Yeah, we are looking pretty good."

"Good?" Ash echoed in mock astonishment. "Dude, if this isn't a World Series–winning team, I don't know what is."

For the base-running exercise, players swung an imaginary bat and then legged it to first. The coaches called out different run patterns, telling them to run through the base, swing wide, or curl around toward second.

"We'll finish up our fieldwork with some position-specific drills," Mr. Harrison informed them when all the players had gone through the line three times.

"Carter, Allen, Luke, and Peter, you'll be doing some pitching in just a bit. For now, pair off and throw lightly to one another while your catchers get in some blocking practice."

Carter stopped by the water jug before retrieving his glove. As he drank, he watched Ash drop to his knees and stop the incoming hoppers over and over. Ash recovered each ball a split second later, tossed it back to Coach Filbert, and then just as quickly returned to his ready position.

He's just as good as Liam, he suddenly thought. *He didn't start out that way at the beginning of the season. But he is now.* He wondered then if Liam had improved, too—although whether his cousin would be playing catcher on his All-Star team was still unknown.

"Everything all right?"

Carter jumped. He'd been so lost in thought he hadn't heard Coach Harrison approach. "Yes, sir," he replied as the coach filled his cup. "I was just thinking about Liam."

The coach took a long drink and wiped his mouth. "I was pleased to hear he made the All-Stars out there in sunny California," he said. "Although when I heard who his teammate was, I admit I was a little taken aback. Think he'll be okay with that DiMaggio boy?"

Carter crumpled his cup and threw it into the trash. "I'll have to get back to you on that one, Coach. He hasn't had his first practice yet."

"I'm sure he'll be fine," the coach said. "Give him my best."

"I will." *And I hope you're right about him being fine,* he added silently, *because the last thing he needs is another curveball.*

CHAPTER
TWENTY-SEVEN

Melanie," Liam cried, "I don't want you filming this practice! Mom!"

Mrs. McGrath hurried into the living room. "What now?"

"She says she has to video everything about my All-Star team if she's going to get a good grade on her summer project," Liam said angrily. "But I don't want her there today."

"Mom," Melanie said, pitching her voice in a reasonable tone, "I have to have hours of footage to create fifteen minutes of really good stuff." Her eyes slid to her brother. "And today promises to have some really good stuff."

When Liam had found out he'd made the All-Star team, he'd been over the moon. But as the first practice drew near, the reality of his situation began to sink in. He was on a team with Phillip DiMaggio. Did he really want his and Phillip's first practice, their first meeting as teammates, to be captured on film?

No, he did not.

"Melanie," their mother said warningly. "Put yourself in Liam's place for a moment."

"Hey, this whole thing was his idea," she reminded them.

"I never told you to make it your summer project," Liam retorted. "That was your idea."

Unlike most schools that issued summer reading lists to students, Melanie's school asked them to return in the fall with a completed art project. They could paint a picture, compose a song, write a one-act play, choreograph a dance, film an animated short—anything so long as it was original and had administrative approval.

Melanie had decided to make a documentary featuring Liam's Little League All-Star team. "I can do profiles of the players, their families, the coaches, the umpires, throw in a little baseball history, and of course get footage of the games. And think of the drama if your team goes all the way to the World Series!"

"We could splat in Districts, you know," Liam had told her. "That'd make for a really short film."

Melanie waved away his concerns. "I have faith in you, little brother. You'll make it at least to Sectionals."

Liam had been secretly flattered that she wanted to make his team the star of her project. He'd been happy for her that Little League had given its approval and that all his new teammates—even Phillip—and their parents had signed the necessary permission forms. But he hadn't counted on her being there for his first encounter with Phillip—or on her persistence.

"Please, Liam," she pleaded. "You won't even know I'm there. You can see everything I record. If you don't want me to use something, I won't. You get final say. Please?"

Liam threw up his hands. "Okay, fine! I give up. But if I see one thing in your movie that I said couldn't be there—"

She put her hand to her heart. "You won't. I promise. I'll go get my equipment."

After she left, Mrs. McGrath said, "Speaking of equipment, do we need to load yours into the trunk?"

Liam hesitated. Dr. Driscoll, the All-Star coach,

hadn't told him if he was playing catcher or not. "I guess we should," he decided. "Better to have it and not need it, than need it and not have it."

"Now who sounds like a fortune cookie?" Melanie said, coming down the stairs with her camera bag.

Fifteen minutes later, they arrived at the field. Melanie told Liam to wait in the car while she set up.

"Great idea. Film me getting out of the car. That should keep the audience spellbound," he said sarcastically as he slid from the seat and slammed the door.

Mrs. McGrath laughed. "Text or call when you're ready to be picked up," she reminded them after Liam had pulled his stuff from the trunk.

Liam nodded and then began to lug his gear bag toward the field. Melanie, camera held high, walked backward, recording his every step.

"Liam McGrath is about to have his first practice with his new Southern California All-Star teammates. One teammate is his friend Rodney Driscoll, who beat him out for the top spot on the home run leaderboard in the regular season." She lowered her voice dramatically. "Another is his rival, Phillip DiMaggio, who threw the pitch that led to Liam's infamous strikeout in the U.S. Championship in last year's World Series tournament. Former rivals now thrown together—can they overcome their differences and work together? Stay tuned!"

She moved the camera aside and grinned. "What do you think of it so far?"

"I think you're in my way." He nudged her—and then froze.

Standing in front of the dugout, feet planted on the ground and fists on hips, was Phillip DiMaggio. Behind Phillip were several other teammates. They'd been chatting and laughing, but when they saw Liam and Phillip staring at each other, they fell silent.

"Here we go," Liam heard Melanie whisper as she began filming again.

Liam hesitated, but only for a second. Then he let go of his equipment sack and started forward. He knew whatever happened in the next minute would affect not just him and Phillip but the whole team. A million ways to handle the situation raced across his brain. Only one stopped and stayed.

"Hey, DiMaggio," he said when he was a few feet away. "I've got something to say to you."

Phillip's eyes narrowed dangerously. "Yeah? And what's that?"

Liam was now face-to-face with the pitcher. The tension was so real that he could almost see a crackle of electricity snap between them. Neither moved a muscle for a long moment.

"It's something I should have said a long time ago," Liam said. Then he stuck out his hand. "Congratulations on winning the World Series."

CHAPTER
TWENTY-EIGHT

Go, Forest Park! Go!"

Rachel's cry rang out loud and clear across the base-ball field. Carter grinned at Ash. "Weird hearing her yell from the bleachers instead of the dugout, isn't it?"

Ash made a face. "I don't mind the change!"

"Come on," Carter chided. "She was a really good player and teammate, and you know it."

"Yeah, okay," Ash grumbled. "She is a great fan," he added when Rachel gave another shout-out to their squad.

The Forest Park All-Star team was about to play its first District game. The opponent was Lakeville. It was a five-day, double-elimination tournament involving five teams. Once a team lost twice, it was out of the competition.

Carter and his teammates had no intention of losing even one.

The game kicked off with the singing of the national anthem. Then Forest Park took to the field for the first inning. Carter was on the mound. Ash was behind the plate. Their new teammates fanned out to their positions. The ball rocketed around the horn, and then it was time to start.

"Play ball!"

Carter accepted the ball from the umpire and stared down at the first batter. Ash flashed the signal for a fastball. Carter nodded, then wound up, reared back, lunged forward, and threw.

Swish!

Thud!

"Strike one!"

That was a call Carter heard many times in the three innings he pitched. When he was replaced at the top of the fourth by Forest Park's closer, Peter Molina, the score was Forest Park 6, Lakeville 3. Each team added a run to the scoreboard, but for Lakeville, it wasn't enough. Carter and his All-Star teammates won, 7–4.

They won the next game, too, but dropped their third to a very tough team from Wolfboro. Their fourth game was a rematch with Lakeville. Knowing the winner would advance to the final and the loser would be eliminated, both teams played their hardest.

It was neck and neck until the top of the sixth, when Craig came up to bat. During the regular season, Carter had been impressed by how much Craig had improved at the plate, and Craig did not disappoint now. He waited for a pitch he liked—and then demolished it, smacking it deep into left field for the tournament's only home run.

The next afternoon, the boys from Forest Park faced the Wolfboro team for the District Championship.

"Okay, boys, this is it," Coach Harrison said. "Win this, and we're on our way to Sectionals!"

"And from Sectionals to State," Ash added excitedly, "to Regionals and then to the World Series!"

"Gotta focus on this one first," Carter advised. "One step at a time, just like always."

"The game's about to start. Hands together, team," Coach Walker said. "Now let's hear it!"

"Forest Park, one-two-three! Forest Park, one-two-three!" the boys and coaches chanted.

Their fans joined in. Carter's parents, Rachel, the Delaneys, and dozens more were all rooting for their favorite team.

Throughout the tournament, Carter's coaches had carefully monitored the pitch counts of each hurler on the team. Luke had pitched the entire game against Lakeville the day before, so, per Little League rules, he was not allowed to pitch in the final. Carter had started the game against Wolfboro two days earlier, but Peter had pitched the bulk of it. Now Peter would start at shortstop and pitch only in the final innings against Wolfboro, and then only if Carter reached his allotted count and needed to come out.

Carter had no intention of being replaced. He intended to pitch the Forest Park All-Stars to victory. The night before, he and Ash studied the information Ash had compiled on Wolfboro, focusing specifically on the batters.

"He's their biggest hitter," Carter said, pointing to the name *Joe Nickerson*. "He likes fastballs." He looked at Ash and raised his eyebrows. "Wonder if he likes *knuckleballs*, though."

Before the game, they talked to Coach Harrison about using the pitch. He nodded approvingly. "You boys read my mind," he said. "I was planning to send in that signal when he was at bat."

Joe Nickerson was Wolfboro's cleanup batter. But there was nothing to clean up in the first inning because Carter mowed down the first three hitters in order. Joe threatened at the start of the second with a soaring blast to right field. But Ash had warned his teammates to be ready—and they were. Instead of getting on base, Joe flied out.

When the Wolfboro heavy hitter got up the next time, there was fire in his eyes. Carter met fire with fire, however, and burned him on two pitches. Ash called for time and hurried to the mound.

"Get him out on the knuckleball?" he asked.

Carter glanced at the coach. "Only if he says to. But I think I can wipe him away with a changeup."

Coach Harrison must have agreed, because that's the signal he sent in. That's the pitch Carter threw. And that's the pitch Joe missed for strike three.

In the dugout, Mr. Harrison beckoned Carter and Ash over. "I suspect Nickerson will be gunning for you next time he's up," he said. "That's when you'll bring out your secret weapon. Okay?"

Carter's adrenaline surged. "Yes, sir!"

The score was Forest Park 4, Wolfboro 3 in the bottom of the fifth inning when Joe came to the plate again. There was one out, runners on first and second, and an expectant smile on the batter's lips.

Think you're going to earn a ribbie? Guess again, Carter thought. He plucked the ball from his glove and hurled it back into the pocket. Over and over, harder and harder, until Joe stepped into the box.

Ash adjusted his crouch. He flashed the signal for a fastball low and outside. Carter threw, and Joe swung and clipped the ball foul for strike one. Twice more, Carter threw the same pitch and twice more Joe nicked it. After the third time, he stepped out of the box and looked at his coach.

When he stepped back in, he stood closer to the plate. Not by much, but enough so that if Carter threw low and outside again, he could hit the ball squarely.

Carter almost grinned when Ash flashed the signal. One-three-four-two. One was a changeup. Two was a two-seam fastball. Three was a four-seam fastball. And four was a knuckleball.

Get ready, Nickerson, he thought, *because I'm about to knock your socks off!*

CHAPTER
TWENTY-NINE

And did you?" Liam asked between bites of his apple.

"See for yourself!" Carter held up a photo showing the Forest Park All-Stars. Across the top was a banner proclaiming them the District Champions.

"I don't like to brag—"

"And yet you're about to."

"—but my knuckleball totally jammed him!" Carter finished proudly.

"I'm so psyched for you, man," Liam said. He peered more closely at the photo. "Which one is Ashley?"

Carter pointed to a blond-haired boy sitting next to him in the photo. "And his name's Ash."

Liam grunted. "Wish it was me in that photo."

Carter put the picture away. "Me too," he murmured. "How's it been with Phillip, anyway?"

Liam seesawed his hand in the air. After he had congratulated Phillip that first practice, the two had settled into an unspoken and uneasy truce for the good of the team. "All right, I guess. I haven't been playing catcher, so I don't work with him all the time."

Carter nodded. "That was a great catch you made in the outfield last game. Maybe I should get someone to film my games so you can see the action over here, too."

Liam made a face. "If I could find a big enough box, I'd ship Melanie to you overnight."

Carter laughed. "Seriously, though, I bet it's going to be a cool movie." He waggled his eyebrows. "How much of the postseason do you think it's going to cover, anyway?"

Liam pressed his fingertips to his temples and intoned in a spooky voice, "The great McGrath predicts...mmmm, ooooo, mmmm...that we will go all the way!" Then in his normal voice, he added, "But first we have to win back-to-back games tomorrow."

Carter clucked his tongue. "Man, a District doubleheader. That's tough."

"Yeah, no kidding. But rules are rules, and when the thunder and lightning started today, they had to cancel all the games." Liam grinned. "District doubleheader—

that has a nice ring to it. Maybe Melanie can use it for the title of her film."

"I thought you were going all the way?"

"Oh, the team is, for sure," Liam said grandly. "But if she doesn't stop sticking that camera in my face, she'll be through after tomorrow!"

The storm that had shut down the fields the day before had long since passed when Liam's All-Star team arrived. Their white jerseys emblazoned in royal blue with their team name, Ravenna, looked blindingly bright in the morning sun. Liam knew that they'd be good and dirty before long, though.

The two games bumped from the previous day were scheduled to take place simultaneously on separate fields. Then, in the early evening, the winners would face each other in the District Championship. With such a busy day, the umpires made sure all teams were ready to begin on time.

"Go get 'em, bro!" Sean Driscoll called to Rodney as Ravenna ran onto the field.

"Yeah, go get 'em, bro!" Melanie echoed, shooting Sean a huge grin.

Then together they yelled, "Go get 'em, Ravenna!"

And that's just what Ravenna did. When the dust

settled, they had plastered their opponents from Sinclair, ten runs to three. Liam had made the final out with a throw from center field to home.

"That play won't end up on the cutting-room floor," Melanie said, patting her camera happily.

The first game ended at noon, so the players returned to their homes to shower and eat.

"Nothing too heavy or greasy or fatty or—oh, what am I saying?" Coach Driscoll grinned. "You're boys. You can eat practically anything and still be ready to go!"

But it turned out that wasn't true. When Ravenna gathered in the dugout for the second game of the doubleheader, Owen Berg was missing. The coach received a call from Mrs. Berg. When he hung up, he had bad news.

"Owen has been sick all afternoon," he informed the team grimly. "She thinks it's something he ate. So he won't be playing today. Which means we need to make some changes to the lineup."

Liam's heart skipped a beat. Owen was supposed to catch that game. Luis Cervantes, Ravenna's other starting catcher, had played the entire first game and needed a rest. That left two possible players for the spot: Cole Dudley—and him.

Pick me, he silently begged. *Give me a chance.*

Liam waited for an agonizing five minutes as the

coaches put their heads together to talk it over. Finally, he had his answer.

"Liam," Coach Driscoll said. "You're behind the plate." Liam was about to give a quiet cheer when the coach added, "Go warm up with Phillip."

The dugout fell silent. Phillip and Liam exchanged glances. Then Phillip grabbed his glove and hurried to the bull pen. Liam, his mind racing, suited up quickly and trotted over to join him.

"Listen, DiMaggio—" he started to say.

"No, you listen," Phillip cut in sharply. Then he shook his head and blew out his breath. "Sorry, that came out wrong. But I guess that's pretty much the way things usually are with us, huh? *Wrong*. But—"

"Not today," Liam finished. "Not this game. This game, we get everything right."

Phillip stared at him. Then he nodded. "Exactly."

They didn't say another word, just got into their positions. Liam hadn't caught for Phillip often. He wished they had more time to find their rhythm now. But they didn't, because Coach Driscoll was calling to them to hit the field.

And then the game that would make or break Ravenna's postseason run began with the umpire's cry.

"Play ball!"

ASIA-PACIFIC REGION (serving all of Asia and
Australia)
Asia-Pacific Regional Director
C/O Hong Kong Little League
Room 1005, Sports House
1 Stadium Path
Causeway Bay, Hong Kong
E-MAIL: bhc368@netvigator.com

EUROPE, MIDDLE EAST & AFRICA REGION
(serving all of Europe, the Middle East, and Africa)
Little League Europe
Al. Meleg Legi 1
Kutno, 99-300, Poland
E-MAIL: Europe@LittleLeague.org

LATIN AMERICA REGION (serving Mexico and Latin
American regions)
Latin America Little League Headquarters
PO Box 10237
Caparra Heights, Puerto Rico 00922-0237
E-MAIL: LatinAmerica@LittleLeague.org

ANSWERS

1. b—Carl E. Stotz first came up with the idea of fielding youth baseball teams in 1938. In 1939, he founded Little League Baseball with the help of the Williamsport, Pennsylvania, community.

2. d—Allen "Sonny" Yearick was a member of the 1939 Lycoming Dairy squad, one of the first three Little League teams. In 1947, he was signed by the Boston Braves. He spent his five-year professional career playing for different farm leagues.

3. c—Thanks to Ed Yonkin's no-hitter, his team, Lundy Lumber, beat Stein's Service. The other players listed also posted Little League Baseball firsts: Fred Shapiro pitched the first perfect game in the Little League Baseball World Series in 1956. In 1957, Angel Macias of Mexico threw the only perfect game in the Series Championship, marking the first time a team from outside the United States won the title. Kiyoshi Tsumura of Japan helped his team get to the 1976 finals by pitching a perfect game in the semifinals. (Japan went on to win its third title.)

4. a—Originally dubbed the National Little League Tournament, the name was later changed to the Little League Baseball World Series after Major League Baseball's World Series. Today, the official name for the tournament is the Little League Baseball World Series.

5. d—The team from Montreal, Quebec, Canada, was beaten in the quarterfinals, 13–7, by Hackensack, New Jersey. The first chartered Little Leagues outside the United States were on each end of the Panama Canal in 1950.

6. d—Victoria Roche played on a team from Brussels, Belgium. Several instances have been recorded of girls playing Little League: In 1950, Kathryn Johnston pretended to be a boy in order to play. Maria Pepe's desire to play baseball spawned the organization to open its doors to girls in 1974. Begining in 2009, pitcher Chelsea Baker wowed fans and opponents with her amazing knuckleball.

7. b—To date, Taiwan has won seventeen Little League Baseball World Series. Japan holds second place, with eight championships; California is in third, with seven.

8. d—President George W. Bush is a lifelong fan of Little League. He played for the Cubs of Midland, Texas. In 2001, Little League's Southwestern Region Headquarters was renamed in his honor. Other former Little Leaguers turned politicians include vice president Joe Biden, vice president Dan Quayle, and senator Bill Bradley.

9. c—Hurricane Irene threatened the Williamsport, Pennsylvania, area with fierce winds and heavy rains. Concerned for the safety of players and fans, Little League chose to move the start of the 2011 Championship Game up from three o'clock Sunday, August 28, to noon that same day.

10. a—The Little League Intermediate 50/70 Baseball Division was created as a bridge between the Little League Division Major and the Teenage. It takes its name from the longer fifty-foot pitching distance and seventy-foot base paths (the Majors' pitching distance is forty-six feet and the base paths are sixty feet) and is open to players ages 11 to 13. The rules more closely follow those of the Junior Baseball Division.